The Road to Cana

CHRIST THE LORD

The Road to Cana

A Novel

ANNE RICE

ALFRED A. KNOPF
New York • Toronto
2008

THIS IS A BORZOI BOOK
PUBLISHED BY ALFRED A. KNOPF
AND ALFRED A. KNOPF CANADA

Copyright © 2008 by Anne O'Brien Rice
All rights reserved. Published in the United States by Alfred A. Knopf,
a division of Random House, Inc., New York, and
in Canada by Alfred A. Knopf Canada, a division of Random House
of Canada, Limited, Toronto.

Knopf, Borzoi Books, and the colophon are registered trademarks
of Random House, Inc.
Knopf Canada and colophon are trademarks.

ISBN 978-1-4000-4352-1

This is a work of fiction. Names, characters, places, and incidents either are
the products of the author's imagination or are used fictitiously.

Manufactured in the United States of America

Invocation.
In the name of the Father,
And of the Son,
And of the Holy Spirit.
Amen.

The truth of the faith can be preserved only by doing a theology of Jesus Christ, and by redoing it over and over again.

—Karl Rahner

O Lord, the one God, God the Trinity, whatsoever I have said in these books is of you, may those that are yours acknowledge; whatsoever of myself alone, do you and yours forgive.

—St. Augustine

In the beginning was the Word, and the Word was with God, and the Word was God.
The same was in the beginning with God.
All things were made by him; and without him was not any thing made that was made.
In him was life; and the life was the light of men.
And the light shineth in darkness; and the darkness comprehended it not.

. . .

He was in the world, and the world was made by him, and the world knew him not.

—The Gospel of John

The Road to Cana

I

Who is Christ the Lord?

Angels sang at his birth. Magi from the East brought gifts: gold, frankincense, and myrrh. They gave these gifts to him, and to his mother, Mary, and the man, Joseph, who claimed to be his father.

In the Temple, an old man gathered the babe in his arms. The old man said to the Lord, as he held the babe, "A light for revelation to the Gentiles, and glory for your people Israel."

My mother told me those stories.

That was years and years ago.

Is it possible that Christ the Lord is a carpenter in the town of Nazareth, a man past thirty years of age, and one of a family of carpenters, a family of men and women and children that fill ten rooms of an ancient house, and, that in this winter of no rain, of endless dust, of talk of trouble in Judea, Christ the Lord sleeps in a worn woolen robe, in a room with other men, beside a smoking brazier? Is it possible that in that room, asleep, he dreams?

Yes. I know it's possible. I am Christ the Lord. I know. What I must know, I know. And what I must learn, I learn.

And in this skin, I live and sweat and breathe and groan. My shoulders ache. My eyes are dry from these dreadful rainless days—from the long walks to Sepphoris through the gray fields in which the seeds burn under the dim winter sun because the rains don't come.

I am Christ the Lord. I know. Others know, but what they know they often forget. My mother hasn't spoken a word on it for years. My foster father, Joseph, is old now, white haired, and given to dreaming.

I never forget.

And as I fall asleep, sometimes I'm afraid—because my dreams are not my friends. My dreams are wild like bracken or sudden hot winds that sweep down into the parched valleys of Galilee.

But I do dream, as all men dream.

And so this night, beside the brazier, hands and feet cold, under my cloak, I dreamed.

I dreamed of a woman, close, a woman, mine, a woman who became a maiden who became in the easy tumult of dreams my Avigail.

I woke. I sat up in the dark. All the others lay sleeping still, with open mouths, and the coals in the brazier were ashes.

Go away, beloved girl. This is not for me to know, and Christ the Lord will not know what he does not want to know— or what he would know only by the shape of its absence.

She wouldn't go—not this, the Avigail of dreams with hair tumbled down loose over my hands, as if the Lord had made her for me in the Garden of Eden.

No. Perhaps the Lord made dreams for such knowing— or so it seemed for Christ the Lord.

I climbed up off the mat, and quietly as I could, I put more coals into the brazier. My brothers and my nephews didn't stir. James was off with his wife tonight in the room they shared. Little Judas and Little Joseph, fathers both, slept here tonight away from little ones huddled around their wives. And there lay the sons of James—Menachim, Isaac, and Shabi, tumbled together like puppies.

I stepped over one after another and took a clean robe from the chest, the wool smelling of the sunshine in which it had been dried. Everything in that chest was clean.

I took the robe and went out of the house. Blast of cold air in the empty courtyard. Crunch of broken leaves.

And for a moment in the hard pebbly street I stopped and looked up at the great sweep of glittering stars beyond the huddled rooftops.

Cloudless, this cold sky, and so filled with these infinitesimal lights, it seemed for a moment beautiful. My heart hurt. It seemed to be looking at me, enfolding me—a thing of kindness and witness—an immense web flung out by a single hand—rather than the vast inevitable hollow of the night above the tiny slumbering town that spilled like a hundred others down a slope between distant caves of bones and thirsting fields, and groves of olive trees.

I was alone.

Somewhere far down the hill, near the sometime marketplace, a man sang in a low drunken voice and a spark of light shone there, in the doorway of the sometime tavern. Echo of laughter.

But all the rest was quiet, without a torch to light the way.

The house of Avigail across from ours was shut up like any other. Inside, Avigail, my young kinswoman, slept with Silent Hannah, her sweet companion, and the two old women who served her and the bitter man, Shemayah, who was her father.

Nazareth did not always have a beauty. I'd seen generations of young maidens grow up, each fresh and lovely to behold as any flower in the wild. Fathers did not want their daughters to be beauties. But Nazareth had a beauty now, and it was Avigail. She'd refused two suitors of late, or so her father had done on her behalf, and there was a real question in the minds of the women of our house as to whether Avigail herself even knew the suitors had come calling.

It fell hard on me suddenly that I would sometime very soon be standing among the torchbearers at her wedding. Avigail was fifteen. She might have been married a year ago, but Shemayah kept her close. Shemayah was a rich man who had but one thing and one thing alone that made him happy, and that was his daughter, Avigail.

I walked up the hill and over the top. I knew every family behind every door. I knew the few strangers who came and went, one huddled in a courtyard outside the Rabbi's house, and the other on the roof above where so many slept, even in winter. It was a town of day-to-day quiet, and seemingly not a single secret.

I walked down the other side of the slope until I came to the spring, the dust rising with every step I took, until I was coughing from it.

Dust and dust and dust.

Thank You, Father of the Universe, that this night is not so cold, no, not as cold as it might be, and send us the rain in Your own good time because You know that we need it.

Passing the synagogue, I could hear the spring before I saw it.

The spring was drying up, but for now it still ran, and it filled the two large rock-cut basins in the side of the hill, and spilled down in glistening streaks to the rocky bed it followed off and away into the distant forest.

The grass grew soft here and fragrant.

I knew that in less than an hour, the women would be coming, some to fill jugs, others, the poorer women, to wash their clothes here as best they could and beat them on the rocks.

But for now the spring was mine.

I stripped off the old robe and flung it down into the creek bed where the water soon filled it up and darkened it to where I couldn't see it. I set the clean robe aside and approached the basin. With my cupped hands I bathed in the cold water, drenching my hair, my face, my chest, letting it run down my back and my legs. Yes, cast away the dreams like the old robe, and bathe them away. The dream woman has no name now and no voice, and what it was, that painful flicker when she laughed or reached out, well, that was gone, fading, like the night itself was fading, and gone too was the dust for this moment, the suffocating dust. There was only cold. There was only water.

I lay down on the far bank, opposite the synagogue. The birds had begun, and as always I'd missed the exact moment. It was a game I played, trying to hear the very first of the birds, the birds that knew the sun was coming when no one else did.

I could see the big thick palm trees around the synagogue emerging from the clump of shapeless shadows. Palms could grow in a drought. Palms didn't care if the dust coated every branch. Palms went on as if made for all seasons.

The cold was outside me. I think my beating heart kept me warm. Then the first light seeped up over the distant bluff, and I picked up the fresh robe, and slipped it over my head. So good, this, this luxuriously clean cloth, this fresh-smelling cloth.

I lay back down again and my thoughts drifted. I felt the breeze before I heard the trees sigh with it.

Far up the hill was an old olive grove to which I loved to

go at times to be alone. I thought of it now. How good it would be to lie in that soft bed of dead leaf and sleep the day away.

But there was no chance of it, not now with the tasks that had to be done, and with the village charged with new worries and new talk over a new Roman Governor come to Judea, who, until he settled in as every other Governor had done, would trouble the land from one end to the other.

The land. When I say the land, I mean Judea and Galilee as well. I mean the Holy Land, the Land of Israel, the Land of God. It was no matter that this man didn't govern us. He governed Judea and the Holy City where the Temple stood, and so he might as well have been our King instead of Herod Antipas. They worked together, these two, Herod Antipas, the ruler of Galilee, and this new man, Pontius Pilate, whom men feared, and beyond Jordan Herod Philip ruled and worked with them as well. And so the land had been carved up for a long, long time, and Antipas and Philip we knew, but Pontius Pilate we didn't know and the reports were already evil.

What could a carpenter in Nazareth do about it? Nothing, but when there was no rain, when men were restive and angry and full of fear, when people spoke of the curse of Heaven on the withering grass, and Roman slights, and an anxious Emperor gone into exile in mourning for a son poisoned, when all the world seemed filled with the pressure to put one's shoulder to it and push, well, in such a time, I didn't go off to the grove of trees to sleep the day away.

It was getting light.

A figure broke from the dark shapes of the houses of the village, hurrying downhill towards me, one hand upraised.

My brother James. Older brother—son of Joseph and Joseph's first wife who died before Joseph married my mother. No mistaking James, for his long hair, knotted at the back of his neck and streaming down his back, and his narrow anxious shoulders and the speed with which he came, James the Nazirite, James, the captain of our band of workers, James, who now in Joseph's old age was head of the family.

He stopped at the far side of the little spring, mostly a broad swatch of dry stones now with the glittering ribbon of water gurgling through the center of it, and I could plainly make out his face as he stared at me.

He stepped on one big stone after another as he came across the creek to me. I had sat up and now I climbed to my feet, a common enough courtesy for my older brother.

"What are you doing out here?" he demanded. "What's the matter with you? Why do you always worry me?"

I didn't say anything.

He threw up his hands and looked to the trees and the fields for an explanation.

"When will you take a wife?" he asked. "No, don't stop me, don't put up your hand to me to silence me. I will not be silenced. When will you take a wife? Are you wed to this miserable creek, to this cold water? What will you do when it runs dry, and it will this year, you know."

I laughed under my breath.

He went right on.

"There are two men as old as you in this town who've never married. One is crippled. The other's an idiot, and everyone knows this."

He was right. I was past thirty and not married.

"How many times have we talked about this, James?" I asked.

It was a beautiful thing to watch the growing light, to see the color coming to the palms clustered around the synagogue. I thought I heard shouting in the distance. But perhaps it was just the usual noises of a town tearing off its blankets.

"Tell me what's really eating at you this morning?" I asked. I picked up the wet robe from the stream and spread it out on the grass where it would dry. "Every year you come to look more like your father," I said, "but you never have your father's face really. You never have his peace of mind."

"I was born worried," he confessed with a shrug. He was looking anxiously towards the village. "Do you hear that?"

"I hear something," I said.

"This is the worst dry spell we've ever had," he said, glancing up at the sky. "And cold as it is, it's not cold enough. You know the cisterns are almost empty. The mikvah's almost empty. And you, you are a constant worry to me, Yeshua, a constant worry. You come out here in the dark to the creek. You go off to that grove where no one dares to go. . . ."

"They're wrong about that grove," I said. "Those old stones mean nothing." That was a village superstition, that something pagan and dreadful had once taken place in that grove. But it was the mere ruins of an old olive press in there, stones that went way back to the years before Nazareth had been Nazareth. "I tell you this once a year, don't I? But I don't want to worry you, James."

2

I EXPECTED JAMES TO CONTINUE.

But he'd gone quiet, staring in the direction of the village.

People were shouting, a lot of people.

I ran my fingers through my hair to smooth it, and turned and looked.

As the full light of day came down, I saw a great cluster of them at the top of the hill, men and boys tumbling and pushing at one another, the whole throng moving slowly downhill towards us.

Out of the melee, the Rabbi emerged, old Jacimus, and, with him, his young nephew Jason. I could see the Rabbi was trying to stop the crowd, but he was swept towards the foot of the hill, towards the synagogue, as the crowd came on, like a frantic herd, until they stopped in the clearing before the palm trees.

As we stood on the slope across the stream we could see them clearly.

Out of their midst, they forced two young boys—Yitra bar Nahom, and beside him the brother of Silent Hannah, the one we all called simply the Orphan.

The Rabbi ran up the stone steps to the roof of the synagogue.

I moved forward, but James held me back harshly.

"Stay out of this," he said.

Rabbi Jacimus' words rang out over the noise of the stream and the grumbling of the crowd.

"We will have a trial here, I tell you!" he demanded. "And I want the witnesses, where are the witnesses? The witnesses will step forward and declare what they saw."

Yitra and the Orphan stood apart as if an impassable gulf separated them from the angry villagers, some of whom were shaking their fists while others cursed under their breath, the oaths that don't require words to convey their meaning.

Again, I moved forward, but James pulled me back. "Stay out of it," he said. "I knew this would happen."

"What? What are you saying?" I demanded.

The crowd broke into shouts and roars. Fingers were pointed. Someone cried out: "Abomination."

Yitra, the older of the two accused, stood still glowering at those before him. He was a righteous boy whom everyone loved, one of the best in the school, and when he'd been taken to the Temple last year, he'd made the Rabbi proud in his answers to the teachers.

The Orphan, smaller than Yitra, was pale with fear, his black eyes huge, and his mouth trembling.

Jason, the Rabbi's nephew, Jason the Scribe, stepped forward on the roof and repeated his uncle's declarations.

"Stop this madness now!" he declared. "There will be a trial according to the law, and you witnesses, where are you? Are you afraid, those of you who started this?"

The crowd drowned out his voice.

Down the hill Nahom, Yitra's father, came running, along with his wife and his daughters. The crowd went into a new wave of insults and invectives, with raised fists and stamping. But Nahom pushed his way through it and looked at his son.

The Rabbi had never stopped calling for this to cease, but we could no longer hear him.

It seemed Nahom spoke to his son, but I couldn't hear it.

And then as the crowd went into a pitch of hatred, Yitra reached out, without thinking perhaps, who could know, and he drew the Orphan protectively to him.

I shouted, "No." But it was lost in the din. I ran forward.

Stones flew through the air. The crowd was a swarming mass beneath the whistling sounds of the stones arching towards the boys in the clearing.

I pushed into the thick of it to get to the boys, James behind me.

But it was finished.

The Rabbi roared like a beast on the roof of the synagogue.

The crowd had gone silent.

The Rabbi, with his hands clasped over his mouth, stared down at the heap of stones below him. Jason shook his head and turned his back.

A howl went up from Yitra's mother, and then came the sobs of his sisters. People turned away. They rushed up the hill, or out to the fields, or over the creek and up the far slope. They fled wherever they could.

And then the Rabbi threw up his arms:

"Run, yes, run from what you've done here! But the Lord on High sees you! The Lord on High sees this!" He balled his fists. "Satan rules in Nazareth!" he bellowed. "Run, run for shame for what you've done, you lawless miserable rabble!" He put his hands to the sides of his head and he began to sob more loudly than Yitra's women. He bent over in his sobbing. Jason held tight to him.

Yitra's women were all gathered and pulled away now by

Nahom. Nahom looked back once and then he dragged his wife up the hill, the girls running after them.

Only the stragglers remained, a few farmhands and odd-job workers, and the children gazing on from their hiding places beneath the palms or in the nearby doors—and James and I staring at the mound of stones, and the two boys who lay there, tumbled together.

Yitra's arm was around the Orphan's shoulder, his head on the Orphan's chest. Blood ran from a cut on the Orphan's head. Yitra's eyes were half closed. No blood except in his hair.

All the life was gone out of them.

I heard the pounding of feet—the last of men rushing away.

Into the clearing next to us came Joseph, and with him Old Rabbi Berekhiah, barely able to walk, and the other white-haired men who made up the elders of the village. My uncles Cleopas and Alphaeus were there. They took their place beside Joseph.

All appeared sleepy, bewildered, and then astonished.

Joseph stared at the dead boys.

"How did this happen?" he whispered. He looked to James and to me.

James sighed. The tears slid down his face. "It was . . . like that," he whispered. "We should have—. I didn't think—." He hung his head.

Above us, on the roof, the Rabbi sobbed onto the shoulder of his nephew who looked away to the open fields, his face the picture of sadness.

"Who accused them?" Uncle Cleopas asked. He looked to me. "Yeshua, who accused them?"

Joseph and Rabbi Berekhiah repeated the question.

"I don't know, Father," I said. "I don't think the witnesses ever came forward."

The Rabbi was choking with sobs.

I moved towards the stones.

Once again, James pulled me back, but this time more gently than before. "Please, Yeshua," he whispered.

I stayed where I was.

I looked at them, the two, lying there as if they were children asleep, amid the heap of stones, and not enough blood between them, really, not enough blood for the Angel of Death even to stop and turn and take notice of them.

3

WE CAME TO THE RABBI'S HOUSE. The doors were open. Jason stood in the far corner against the racks of books, his arms folded. Old Rabbi Jacimus sat hunched over his desk, his elbows on the parchment, his head covered.

He rocked back and forth and he prayed or read, it was impossible to know. Perhaps he didn't know.

" 'Don't be angry with men because we are nothing,' " he whispered. " 'And don't take account of what we do; for what are we?' "

I stood quietly beside Joseph and James, waiting and listening. Cleopas stood behind us.

" 'For behold, by Your will we enter this world, and we don't go out of it by our will; who has ever said to his father and mother, "Beget us." And who goes into the realm of Death saying, "Receive us"? What strength do we have, Lord, to bear Your anger? What are we that we can bear Your justice?' "

He turned; he realized we were there, and then he sat back and sighed and turned a little towards us but went on with his praying. " 'Shelter us in Your grace, and in Your mercy give help to us.' "

Joseph repeated these words softly.

Jason looked for a moment as if all this was beyond his endurance, but there was a wistful softness to his eyes that I'd seldom seen in him. He was a beautiful man with dark hair, always finely dressed, and on the Sabbath his linen robes often gave off the faint scent of frankincense.

The Rabbi, who had been a man in his prime when I'd first come home to Nazareth, was now slightly crippled by his age, and his hair was as white as that of Joseph or my uncles. He looked at us as if we couldn't see him, as if we didn't stand waiting on him, as if he were merely looking from some safe place at us and wondering, and then he said sleepily,

"Are they taken away?" He meant the bodies of the boys.

"They are," Joseph said. "And the bloodied stones with them. All taken."

The Rabbi looked to Heaven and sighed. "They belong now to Azazel," he said.

"No, but they're gone," said Joseph. "And we come to see you. We know you're miserable. What do you want us to do? Shall we go to Nahom and the boy's mother?"

The Rabbi nodded. "Joseph, I want you to stay here and comfort me," he said, shaking his head, "but that's where you belong. Nahom has brothers in Judea. He should take his family and go. He'll never rest easy in this village again. Joseph, tell me, why did this happen?"

Jason roused himself with his usual fire. "One doesn't have to go to Athens and Rome to learn the things those boys did," he said. "Why can't they happen in Nazareth?"

"That's not my question," said the Rabbi, looking sharply at him. "I don't ask about what the boys did. We don't know what the boys did! There was no trial, no witnesses, no justice! I ask how could they stone those boys, that's what I ask. Where is the law, where is justice?"

One might have thought he despised his nephew from the manner in which he'd answered him, but in fact, the Rabbi loved Jason. The Rabbi's sons were dead. Jason kept the Rabbi young, and whenever Jason wasn't in Nazareth the Rabbi was distant and forgetful. As soon as Jason came through the door from some far-off place, with a sack of books over his shoulder, the Rabbi sprang to life, and sometimes in their fiery back-and-forth, the Rabbi seemed a boy in his passion.

"Ah, and what will they do," Jason asked, "when Yitra's father gets hold of the children who started this. And they were children, you know, those little boys who hang around the tavern, and they're gone, they were gone before the first stone flew through the air. Nahom can spend his life looking for those boys."

"Children," said my uncle Cleopas, "children who might not have even known what they saw. What, two young ones under the same blanket on a winter night?"

"It's over," said James. "What, are we to have the trial now that we didn't have before? It's finished."

"You're right," said the Rabbi. "But will you go to the mother and the father, will you do this for me? If I go, I'll weep too much and too long and I'll become angry. If Jason goes, he'll say strange things."

Jason laughed darkly. "Strange things. That this village is a miserable heap of dust? Yes, I would say such strange things."

"You do not have to live here, Jason," said James. "No one ever said Nazareth needed its own Greek philosopher. Go back to Alexandria, or Athens, or Rome, or wherever it is you're always running off to. Do we need your ruminations? We never did."

"James, be patient," said Joseph.

The Rabbi appealed to Joseph as if he hadn't even heard the argument.

"Go to them, Joseph, you and Yeshua, you always know the right words. Yeshua can calm anyone. Explain to Nahom that his son was a child himself and the Orphan, ah the poor Orphan."

We were about to take our leave when Jason came sidling forward and glared at me. I looked up.

"Be careful men don't say the same things of you, Yeshua," he said.

"What are you saying?" the Rabbi declared. He rose out of the chair.

"Never mind," said Joseph quietly. "It's nothing, only Jason in his grief for more things than one can know."

"What, you mean they don't say strange things about Yeshua?" said Jason, staring at Joseph, and then at me. "You know what they call you, my mute and immutable friend," he said to me. "They call you Yeshua, the Sinless."

I laughed, but I turned away so that it didn't seem that I laughed in his face. But I was actually laughing in his face. He went on talking, but I didn't hear him. I fell to watching his hands. He had beautiful smooth hands. And often when he went into a tirade or a long poem, I merely watched his hands. They made me think of birds.

The Rabbi suddenly grabbed at Jason's robe, and swung at him with his right hand as if to slap him. But then he fell back in his chair, and Jason flushed red. Now he was sorry, dreadfully sorry.

"Well, they talk, don't they?" Jason said, looking at me. "Where is your wife, Yeshua, where are your children?"

"I will not stand here and endure this a moment longer," said James. He pulled me toward the street by my arm. "You will not speak this way to my brother," he said to Jason.

"Everyone knows what eats at you. You think we're fools? You can't bear it, can you? Avigail's refused you. Her father laughed you to scorn."

Joseph pushed James out of the room and past me. "Enough, my son. You take the bait every time with him."

Cleopas nodded to this.

The Rabbi slumped in his chair and put his head down on his parchments.

Joseph bent down and whispered to the Rabbi. I heard the consoling tone but not the words. Jason meantime was glaring at James as though James was now his personal enemy, and James was sneering at Jason.

"Is there not enough woe in this village for you?" Cleopas asked him calmly. "Why do you always play the Satan? You have to put my nephew Yeshua on trial because there was no trial for Yitra and the Orphan?"

"Sometimes I think," said Jason, "that I was born to say what others think yet no one will utter. I warn Yeshua, that's all." He dropped his voice to a whisper. "Doesn't his own kinswoman wait on his decision?"

"That's not true!" James declared. "That's the feverish idiocy of an envious mind! She refused you because you're mad, and why would a woman marry the wind, if she doesn't have to?"

Suddenly they were all talking at once, Jason, James, Cleopas, and even Joseph, and the Rabbi.

I went on down the street. The sky was blue and the town was empty. Nobody wanted to come out on account of what had happened. I walked on farther, but I could still hear them.

"Go write a letter to your epicurean friends in Rome," said James in a hard voice. "Tell them of the scandalous goings-on in the miserable hamlet where you're condemned to live. Write a satire, why not?"

He came after me.

Jason came after him, brushing past the older men who followed.

"I'll tell you this much if I do," said Jason furiously. "If I write anything of any value, there's only one man in this place who'll understand what I write and that's your brother, Yeshua."

"Jason, Jason . . ." I said. "Come now, why all this?"

"Well, if it wasn't this, it would be something else," said James. "Don't talk to him. Don't look at him. On a day such as this, he starts a quarrel. It's a bitter winter without rain, and Pontius Pilate threatens to put his ensigns in the Holy City. Yet he wants to fight about this."

"You think that's a joke," Jason railed. "Those ensigns? I tell you those soldiers are marching on Jerusalem right now and they will put those ensigns in the Temple itself if they want to. It's come to that."

"Stop, we do not know any such thing," said Joseph. "We wait on news of Pontius Pilate as we wait on the rain. An end to this, both of you."

"Go back to your uncle," said James. "Why do you follow us and bother us? No one else in Nazareth will talk to you. Go back. Your uncle needs you now. Aren't there pages to be written, to report these hideous goings-on, to somebody? Or is this country lawless as the brigands who live in the hills? What, we just put them in a cave and nothing is recorded of how they died? Go back to your work."

Joseph now gave James a stern look that silenced him, and sent him on ahead with his head bowed.

We went on our way, after him, but Jason followed.

"I don't mean you any harm, Yeshua," he said. His confidential tone was infuriating James, and James turned back, but Joseph stopped him.

"I didn't mean you any harm," Jason repeated. "This

place is cursed. The rain will never come. The fields are drying up. The gardens are withered. The flowers are dead."

"Jason, my friend," I said, "the rain always comes, sooner or later."

"And what if it never does? What if now the windows of Heaven are shut against us and with reason?" A torrent of words was about to break from him. But I put up my hand.

"Come later on, and we'll talk over a cup of wine," I said. "Now I have to be on my way to this family."

He fell back, ambling towards his uncle's door. Then I heard him behind me from a distance,

"Yeshua, forgive me," he said.

He said it loud enough for everyone to hear.

"Jason," I said, "you're forgiven."

4

Yitra's mother had the whole family packing everything into bundles. The donkeys were loaded down. The little ones were rolling up the rug off the dirt floor, the fine rug which had been perhaps their most important single thing.

When Yitra's mother saw Joseph she rose up off her knees and flew into his arms. But she trembled with dry eyes and merely clung to him as if she feared drowning.

"You travel safe to Judea," Joseph said. "Even the journey will do you good, and by nightfall, your little ones will be far away from the whispers and stares of this place. We know where Yitra lies. We'll see to him."

She stared off as if trying to make sense of this.

Then in came Nahom, the father, with two of his hired hands. We could see the hired hands had forced Nahom to come home, and he fell back against the wall, his eyes vacant.

"Never mind those creatures," said Joseph to him. "They've fled. They know they did wrong. Leave them to the mercy of Heaven. You go on to Judea now, and shake the dust of this town off your feet."

One of the hired hands, a gentle sort of man, came forward and nodded as he put his arms around Joseph and

Nahom. "Shemayah's going to buy your land, and he'll send you a good price," he said. "I'd buy it if I could. You go on. Joseph's right, those creatures who accused the boys are far away now. They'll probably find their way to the brigands in the mountains. That's where trash like that often goes. What can you do to them anyway? Can you kill every man in this village?"

Yitra's mother closed her eyes, and her head dropped. I thought she'd faint but she didn't.

Joseph drew them both closer to him.

"You have these little ones now. What will happen to them if you don't stand up to this?" asked Joseph. "Now, listen, I want to tell you . . . I want to tell you. . . ." He faltered. His eyes were welling with tears. He couldn't find his words.

I came close and put my arms on the two of them, and they looked to me suddenly like terrified children.

"There was no trial, as you know," I said. "That means that no one will ever know what Yitra did or the Orphan did, or how it was, or when it was, or if nothing ever happened. No one will know. No one can know. Not even the little boys who accused them knew. Only Heaven knows. Now you mustn't have a trial for the boys in your heart. There can't be one. And that means there should be none. And so you mourn for Yitra in your heart. And Yitra is forever innocent. He has to be. It can't be otherwise, not this side of Heaven."

Yitra's mother looked up at me. Her eyes narrowed and then she nodded. Nahom gave no expression, but slowly he moved to pick up the bundles that remained, and sluggishly he carried them out to the waiting animals.

"We wish you a safe journey," said Joseph, "and now you must tell me if you need anything for the journey. My sons and I will get whatever you need."

"Wait," said Yitra's mother. She went to a chest that lay

on the floor, and undid the fastenings. Out of it she took a folded garment, what might have been a wool mantle.

"This," she said, as she gave it to me. "This is for Silent Hannah."

Silent Hannah was the Orphan's sister.

"You will take care of her, won't you?" the woman asked.

Joseph was amazed.

"My child, my poor child," he said. "So kind of you to think of Silent Hannah at a time such as this. Of course, we'll take care of her. We'll always take care of her."

5

WHEN WE CAME INTO THE HOUSE, we saw Silent Hannah there at once with Avigail.

Now wherever Avigail went, Silent Hannah went, and wherever the two went, there was always a gathering of children. James' sons, Isaac and Shabi, my other nephews and nieces, there was always such a crowd around Avigail and Silent Hannah. It was Avigail who drew the children, often singing to them, teaching them old songs, how to read bits of Scripture, even now and then rhymes that she made up in her head, and letting the little girls help her with her twine and her needles, and all the bits and pieces of mending she usually had in her basket. Silent Hannah, who did not hear or speak, lived with Avigail most of the time, though now and then, if Avigail's father was very sick, with his bad leg, Silent Hannah might lodge with us, with my aunts and my mother.

But now, as we came in, only the women were there with Avigail and Silent Hannah. All the children had been sent away, it was plain, and Silent Hannah stood up at once for news and looked imploringly to Joseph.

Avigail stood ready to support her. Avigail's eyes were red

from crying, and she looked not at all like our Avigail, suddenly, but rather more like a woman in the mold of Yitra's mother. The sorrow of all this had transfigured her face, and she kept her gaze fixed on Silent Hannah and waited.

Now Silent Hannah had fluid and eloquent gestures for everything, and we all knew them. It had been several years since she and the Orphan had come to Nazareth as vagabonds do, and she'd lived with us since that time, and the Orphan had lived in many places. But we all knew her language of signs and I thought her hands as beautiful sometimes as Jason's hands.

No one knew how old she was. She might have been fifteen or sixteen. The Orphan had been younger.

Now, she stood before Joseph and very suddenly she broke into the gestures that signified her brother. Where was her brother? What had happened to her brother? No one would tell her. Her eyes swept the room, swept the faces of the women against the walls. What happened to her brother?

Joseph started to answer her. He started but once again the tears came to his eyes, and his pale hands hung in the air, unable to describe the shapes he saw or wanted to see.

James was worried. Cleopas started with words. He didn't know the signs very well. He never had.

Avigail could say and do nothing.

Finally I turned Silent Hannah to me. I made the gesture for her brother, and pointed to my lips, which I knew she could now and then read. I pointed upwards and made the sign for prayer. I talked slowly as I made the various signs.

"The Lord watches over your brother now, and your brother is sleeping. Your brother is asleep in the earth now. You will not see him again." I pointed to her eyes. I leaned forward and pointed then to my own eyes and to Joseph's eyes, and the tears on his face. I shook my head. "Your brother is with the Lord now," I said. I kissed my fingers and gestured again upward.

Silent Hannah's face crumpled and she pulled away from me violently.

Avigail took firm hold of her.

"Your brother will rise on the last day," Avigail said, and she looked upward, and then, letting Silent Hannah go, she made a great encompassing gesture as if the whole world were gathered under Heaven.

Silent Hannah was in terror. She hunched her shoulders and peered at us through her fingers.

I spoke again, gesturing. "It was quick. It was wrong. It was like someone falling. Suddenly over."

I made the gestures for rest, for sleep, for calm. I made them as slowly as I could.

I saw her face slowly change.

"You're our child," I said. "You live with us and with Avigail."

She waited a long moment and then asked Where was her brother laid to rest? I gestured to the far hills, high up in the hills. Silent Hannah knew the caves. She didn't need to know which cave, that it was the cave for those who die by stoning.

Her face was fixed again but only for a moment, and then with a strange fearful expression, she made the gestures for Where is Yitra?

"Yitra's family is gone," I said. I made the gestures for mother and father, and little ones, walking.

She looked at me. She knew this couldn't be right, couldn't be all of it. Again, she made the gesture for Where is Yitra?

"Tell her," said Joseph.

I did. "In the ground, with your brother. Gone now."

Her eyes grew wide with shock. Then, for the first time

ever I saw her lips draw back in a bitter smile. A groan came from her, a terrible tongueless sound.

James sighed. He and Cleopas looked at each other.

"You come on home with me now," said Avigail.

But this wasn't finished.

Joseph quickly gestured to the Heavens again, and made the signs for rest and peace under Heaven.

"Help me with her," said Avigail, because Silent Hannah wouldn't be moved.

My mother and my aunts came forward. Slowly Silent Hannah yielded. She walked as one in a dream. Out of the house they went, the group of them.

She must have stopped in the street. We heard a sound like an ox bellowing, a huge and awful sound. It was Silent Hannah.

By the time I reached her, she'd gone wild, thrashing at everyone around her, kicking, pushing, and out of her came this shapeless bellowing louder and louder, echoing off the walls. She pushed at Avigail and flung Avigail against the wall, and Avigail suddenly broke into sobs and began screaming.

Shemayah, Avigail's father, opened the door.

But Avigail flung herself on Silent Hannah, sobbing and crying and letting the tears run, and pleading with Silent Hannah to please please Come. "Come with me!" Avigail sobbed.

Silent Hannah had stopped her moans. She stood still staring at Avigail. Avigail let herself convulse with her sobs. She threw up her arms and then went down on her knees.

Silent Hannah ran to her and lifted her. Silent Hannah began to comfort her.

All the women gathered around. They stroked the hair of the two young women; they stroked their arms and their shoulders. Silent Hannah kept wiping at Avigail's tears as if she really could wipe them completely away. She clutched Avigail's face and wiped hard at her tears. Avigail nodded. Silent Hannah patted Avigail over and over.

Shemayah held the door open for his daughter, and finally the two young women went into the house together.

We went back into our house. The coals were glowing in the darkness, and someone put a cup of water in my hand, and said, "Sit down."

I saw Joseph against the wall, his ankles crossed, his head bowed.

"Father, you don't come with us today," said James. "You stay here, please, and watch the little ones. They need you here today."

Joseph looked up. For a moment he looked as if he didn't know what James was saying to him. The usual argument did not come. Not even a sound of protest. Then he nodded and closed his eyes.

In the courtyard, James clapped his hands to make the boys hurry. "We mourn in our hearts," he reminded them. "Now we're late. And those of you who work here today, I want this yard swept, do you understand? Look at it." He turned around and around, pointing at the dead dried vines that clung to the lattices, to the leaves heaped in every corner, to the fig tree that was no more now than a tangle of bones.

Once we were on the road, crowded into the usual slow grind of wagons and teams of workers, he drew me close to him and said,

"Did you see what happened to Father? Did you see it? He tried to speak and—."

"James, this day would have wearied any man, but after this . . . he should stay home."

"How can we persuade him of that, that I can run things now? Look at Cleopas. He's dreaming, talking to the fields."

"He knows."

"Everything falls on me."

"It's the way you want it," I said.

Cleopas was my mother's brother. It didn't fall to him to be the head of the family. It was the sons of Cleopas, and his daughter Little Salome, whom I called my brothers and sister. The wives of these brothers were my sisters. The wife of James was my sister.

"That's true," James said with a little surprise. "I do want it all to fall on me. I don't complain. I want things done as they should be done."

I nodded. I said, "You're good at it."

Joseph never went into Sepphoris to work again.

6

Two days passed before I got away to the grove, my grove.

In spite of unceasing work, we'd finished a series of walls early; nothing further could be done until the plaster dried, and so there came an hour of daylight in which I could go off, without a word to anyone, and seek the place I most loved, amid the ancient olive trees and veiled in a tangle of ivy that seemed to thrive in the drought as well as in the rain.

As I said before, the villagers were suspicious of the place and didn't go there. The oldest olives no longer bore fruit, and some were hollowed out, big hulking gray sentinels with wild young trees taking root in their emptied trunks. There were stones there, but I'd years ago satisfied myself that they'd never been a pagan altar or part of a burial ground; and the layer of leaves had long covered them so that the place was soft there for lying, just as an open field might be with silken grass, and in its own way just as sweet.

I had a roll of clean rags with me for a pillow. I crept in and lay down and allowed myself a long slow breath.

I thanked the Lord for this enclosure, for this escape.

I looked up at the play of light in the mesh of faintly

moving branches. The winter days faded abruptly. The sky was already colorless. I didn't mind. I knew the way back home plainly enough. But I couldn't stay as long as I wanted. I'd be missed, and someone would come looking for me, and I would be trouble, and that was not what I wanted to be at all. What I wanted was to be alone.

I prayed; I tried to clear my mind. It was fragrant and wholesome here. It was precious. There was no such place in Nazareth as this, and no such place for me in Sepphoris, or Magdala, or Cana, or anyplace in which we worked or ever would work.

And every room in our house was filled.

Little Cleopas, the grandson of my uncle Alphaeus, had married last year to a cousin, Mary, from Capernaum, and they had taken the last of the rooms, and already Mary was carrying a child.

So I was alone. Just for a little while. Alone.

I tried to shake off the atmosphere of the village, the air of recrimination that had settled on people after the stoning; no one wanted to talk about it, but no one could think of anything else. Who had been there? Who had not? And had those children run off to throw in their lot with the brigands, and somebody ought to seek out those brigands and burn them out of their caves.

And of course the brigands had been raiding the villages. That often happened. And now with the drought the price of food was dear. Rumor had it, the brigands had swept down on the smaller hamlets to steal livestock, and to steal winesacks and sacks of water. No one ever knew when one of these cutthroat men on horseback would come stomping through our streets.

That was very much the talk in Sepphoris, of brigands in a bad winter. But there was also talk everywhere of Pilate and his soldiers moving sluggishly towards Jerusalem with ensigns bearing the name of Caesar, ensigns which should not pass through the city gates. It was blasphemy to bring such ensigns, bearing the name of an Emperor, into our city. We didn't hold with images; we didn't hold with the name or image of an Emperor who held himself to be a god.

Under the Emperor Augustus Caesar nothing like that had ever happened. No one was really certain that Augustus himself had ever believed he was a god. He went along with it, of course, and there were temples reared in his honor. Perhaps his heir Tiberius didn't believe it either.

But people didn't care about the private views of the Emperor. They cared that those ensigns were being carried by Roman soldiers through Judea, and they didn't like it, and the King's soldiers argued about it, too, outside the palace gates and in the taverns, and in the marketplace, or wherever they might happen to be.

The King himself, Herod Antipas, wasn't in Sepphoris. He was in Tiberias, his new city, a city named for the new Emperor, that Herod had built on the sea. We never went to work in that city. A cloud hung over it; graves had been moved to build it. And once the laborers who hadn't cared about such things had flooded east to work there, we had more work in Sepphoris than we could ever want to do.

We'd always done well in Sepphoris. And the King sometimes came to his palace, and whether he did or not, there was an eternal parade of the highborn through his various chambers, and for their splendid houses, the building never stopped.

Now these rich men and women were as worried about the actions of Pontius Pilate as was anyone else. When it came to Romans taking ensigns into the Holy City, Jews of all walks of life were very simply Jews.

Nobody seemed to know this Pontius Pilate; but every-body despised him.

And meantime, word of the stoning had spread through-out the countryside, and people glanced at us as if we were the miserable mob from Nazareth, or so my brothers and nephews thought as they hurled back their own glances, and people disputed over the cost of grout for the bricks I laid, or the thickness of the plaster stirred in the pot.

Of course people were right to be worried about Pontius Pilate. He was new and he didn't know our ways. Rumor had it the man was of the party of Sejanus, and no one had any great love for Sejanus, because Sejanus ran the world, it seemed, for the retired Emperor Tiberius, and who was Sejanus, men said, except a conniving and vicious soldier, a commander of the Emperor's personal guard?

I didn't want to think about these things. I didn't want to think of Silent Hannah's suffering as she came and went with Avigail, clinging to Avigail's arm. Nor did I want to think of the sadness in Avigail's eyes as she looked at me, a darkling understanding that muted her easy laughter and her once fre-quent little songs.

But I couldn't shut these thoughts out of my head. Why had I come to the grove? What had I thought I could find here?

For an instant, I fell asleep. *Avigail. Don't you know this is Eden? It's not good for a man to be alone!*

I woke with a start, in the darkness, bundled up my rags, and went out of the grove to go home.

Far below I saw the twinkling of torches in Nazareth. Winter days meant torches. Men had to work a little while more by lamp or lantern or torch. I found it a cheerful sight.

But where I stood the sky was cloudless, moonless—and beautifully black with the countless stars. "Who can fathom

Your goodness, O Lord?" I whispered. "You have taken the fire and out of it fashioned the numberless lamps that decorate the night."

A stillness came over me. The common ache in my arms and shoulders died away. The breeze was chilling yet soothing. Something inside me let go. It had been a long while since I'd savored such a moment, since I'd let the tight prison of my skin dissolve. I felt as if I were moving upward and outward, as if the night were filled with myriad beings and the rhythm of their song drowned out the anxious beating of my heart. The shell of my body was gone. I was in the stars. But my human soul wouldn't let me loose. I reached for human language. "No, I will accomplish this," I said.

I stood on the dry grass beneath the vault of Heaven. I was small. I was isolated and weary. "Lord," I said aloud to the faint breeze. "How long?"

7

Two lanterns were burning in the courtyard and that was cheerful. I was glad to see it, glad to see my nephew Little Cleopas and his father, Silas, at work on cutting a series of planks. I knew what this was, and it had to be done by tomorrow.

"You look tired, both of you," I said. "Stop now, and I'll do this. I'll cut the wood."

"We can't let you do it," Silas said. "Why should you finish it all alone?" He gestured ominously towards the house. "It has to be done tonight."

"I can do it tonight," I said. "I'm glad to do it. I want to be alone just now with something to do. And Silas, your wife is waiting for you in the doorway. I just saw her. Go on."

Silas nodded and he went off home up the hill. He lived with his wife in the house of our cousin Levi, who was his wife's brother. But Silas' son, Little Cleopas, lived with us.

Little Cleopas gave me a quick embrace and went into the house.

There was plenty of light from the lanterns to see what had to be done here, and the lines drawn had to be perfectly straight. I had the tool for it, the bit of broken pot to mark it. Seven lines to be drawn.

Up came Jason walking into the yard.

His shadow fell over me. I smelled wine.

"You've been avoiding me, Yeshua," he said.

"That's nonsense, my friend," I said. I laughed. I went on with my work. "I've been doing whatever needs to be done. I haven't seen you. Where have you been?"

He paced as he talked. I saw his shadow sharply on the flagstones. He had a cup of wine in his hand. I could hear him take a drink.

"You know where I've been," he said. "How many times have you come up the hill and sat on the floor beside me and insisted I read to you? How many times have I told you the news from Rome and you've hung on every word?"

"That's in summer, Jason, when the days are longer," I said mildly. I carefully drew a straight line.

"Yeshua, the Sinless, you know why I call you this?" he insisted. "It's because everyone loves you, Yeshua, everyone, and no one can bear to love me."

"Not so, Jason. I love you. Your uncle loves you. Almost everyone loves you. You're not hard to love. But sometimes you're hard to understand."

I moved the plank and laid down the next.

"Why doesn't the Lord send rain?" he demanded.

"Why ask me?" I replied, without looking up.

"Yeshua, there are many things I've never told you, things I didn't think bore repeating."

"Perhaps they don't."

"No, I'm not talking about the stupid gossip in this village. I'm talking about other stories, old stories."

I sighed and sat back on my heels. I stared forward beyond him, beyond his slow pacing in the flickering light. He wore beautiful sandals. His sandals were exquisitely made and studded with what appeared to be gold. The tassels of his robe brushed me as he turned and moved like an anxious animal.

"You know I lived with the Essenes," he said. "You know I wanted to be an Essene."

"You've told me," I said.

"You knew I knew your kinsman John bar Zechariah when I lived with the Essenes," he went on. He took another drink.

I decided to try to draw another straight line.

"You've told me this many times, Jason," I said. "Have you had any news from your friends among the Essenes? You'd tell me, wouldn't you, if someone had word of my cousin John."

"Your cousin John's in the wilderness, that's all anyone ever says, in the wilderness, living off the wild things. Nobody's seen him this year at all. Nobody really saw him last year. A man told another man who told another man perhaps he'd seen your cousin John."

I started to draw the line.

"But you know, Yeshua, I never told you everything your cousin told me when I was there living with the community."

"Jason, you have many things on your mind. I scarcely think my cousin John has much to do with it, if he has anything at all." I was trying to draw the line. The line wasn't straight. I took a rag, knotted it, and rubbed at the mark. I'd cut a little too deep, but I kept at it.

"Oh, yes, your cousin John has plenty to do with it," he said, stopping in front of me.

"Move to the left, you're in the light."

He reached around, picked up the lantern by its hook, and set it down right in front of me.

I sat back again, but I didn't look at him. The light was in my eyes.

"All right, Jason, what is it you want to tell me now about my cousin John?"

"I have a mind for poetry, don't I?"

"Without doubt." I rubbed gently at the mark, and watched it slowly fade from the wood. The wood took on a slight luster.

"This is what makes me pick at you," he said, "the words that John entrusted to me, the litanies that he carried in his heart—about you. These litanies he had from his mother's own lips and he recited them each day as he recited the Shema with all Israel, but these litanies were his private prayers. You know what these words were?"

I thought for a moment. "I don't know that I do," I said.

"Very well, then, let me tell you."

"Seems you're determined to do that."

He crouched down now. What a picture he was with his beautifully oiled black hair and his large scowling eyes.

"Before John's birth, your mother came to his mother. She was near Bethany then, and her husband, Zechariah, was still alive. They didn't kill Zechariah till after John was born."

"Yes, this is the story," I said. I went back to trying to draw the line, correctly this time, no mistakes. I cut into the wood with the sharp bit of pottery.

"Your mother told John's mother of the angel who'd come to her," Jason said, leaning close to me.

"Everyone in Nazareth knows that story, Jason," I said, and continued to draw the line.

"No, but your mother," he said, "your mother, standing there in the open space, with her arms around John's mother, your mother, your quiet mother who says so little so seldom, at that moment, she broke into a hymn. She looked beyond to the hills where the prophet Samuel was buried, and from the ancient words of Hannah, she made her hymn."

I stopped my work. I looked up slowly at him.

His voice came reverent and low, and his face was open and kind.

" 'My soul proclaims the greatness of the Lord. My spirit rejoices in God, my Savior. Because He has looked upon the lowliness of His handmaid. Behold, from now on, all ages will call me blessed. The mighty One has done marvelous things for me; and holy is His name. His mercy is from age to age to those who fear Him. He's shown might with His arm, scattering the arrogant of mind and heart. He's thrown down rulers from their thrones but lifted up the humble. The hungry He's filled with good things. The rich He's sent away empty. He has had mercy on Israel His servant, remembering His mercy, according to His promise to our fathers. . . .' "

He stopped.

We looked at one another.

"You know this prayer?" he asked.

I didn't answer.

"Well, then," he said sadly. "I'll tell you another—the prayer spoken by John's father, Zechariah, the priest, when John was given his name."

I said nothing.

" 'Blessed be the Lord, the God of Israel, for He has visited and brought redemption to His people. He has raised up a horn for our salvation within the house of David, His servant, even as He promised through the mouths of the prophets of old.' " He broke off, looking down for a moment. He swallowed and then he went on. " 'Salvation— from our enemies and from the hand of all who hate us . . . and you child'—he spoke here of his son John, you understand—'and you child will be called prophet of the Most High, for you will go before the Lord to prepare His ways. . . .' "

He stopped, unable to go on.

"What's the use of this!" he whispered. He stood up and turned his back.

I took up the words as I knew them.

" 'To give His people knowledge of salvation through the forgiveness of their sins,' " I said. " 'Because of the tender mercy of our Lord.' "

He stared down at me astonished.

I continued, " 'Through which the daybreak from on high will visit us . . . to shine on those who sit in darkness and in the shadow of death, to guide our feet into the path of peace.' "

He drew back, his face blank.

" 'Into the path of peace,' Jason," I said. " 'Into the path of peace.' "

"But where is he, your cousin!" he demanded. "Where is John who is to be the prophet? Pontius Pilate's soldiers are outside Jerusalem tonight. The fires told us so at sunset. What will you do?"

I folded my arms and looked at him, the picture he made in his fervor and his fury. He drank the rest of his wine and set the cup on the bench. It fell off the bench and broke. I stared at it—at the broken pieces. He didn't even see them. He hadn't heard the cup break.

He drew close to me and crouched down again so that his face was fully in the light.

"Do you yourself believe these stories?" he asked. "Tell me; tell me before I go out of my mind."

I didn't answer.

"Yeshua," he pleaded.

"Yes, I believe in them," I said.

He stared expectantly at me for the longest time, but I did nothing.

He put his hands to his head. "Oh, I shouldn't have told you these things. I promised your cousin John I would never reveal these things. I don't know why I did this. I thought . . . I thought . . ."

"This is a bitter time," I said. "Yitra and the Orphan are dead. The sky is the color of the dust. Each day breaks our backs and hurts our hearts."

He looked at me. He wanted so much to understand.

"And we wait on the Lord's tender mercy," I said. "We wait on the Lord's time."

"You're not afraid it's all lies? Yeshua, are you ever afraid that it's all lies?"

"You know the stories that I know," I said.

"Not afraid of what's about to happen in Judea?" he demanded.

I shook my head.

"I love you, Yeshua," he said.

"And I love you, my brother," I said.

"No, don't love me. Your cousin would not forgive me if he knew I talked about these secrets."

"And who is my cousin John that he should live his whole life without ever confiding to a friend?" I asked.

"A bad friend, a restless friend," he replied.

"A friend with much on his mind," I said. "You must have been noisy among the Essenes."

"Noisy!" He laughed. "They threw me out."

"I know," I said. I laughed. Jason loved to tell the story of how the Essenes asked him to leave. It was almost always the first thing he told a new acquaintance, that the Essenes had asked him to go.

I picked up the potsherd and started to cut again, fast, holding the measure perfectly still. Straight line.

"You will not ask for Avigail's hand, will you?" he asked.

"No, I will not," I answered, reaching for the next plank. "I'll never marry." I went on measuring.

"That's not what your brother James says," he answered.

"Jason, leave off," I said gently. "What James says is between him and me."

"He says you will marry her—yes, Avigail—and he will see to it. He says her father will accept you. He says money means nothing to Shemayah. He says you're the man her father won't—."

"Leave off!" I said. I looked up at him. He was towering over me now as if he meant to threaten me.

"What is it?" I asked. "What's really inside you? Why won't you let this go?"

He came down on his knees, and sat back on his heels, so that we were eye to eye again. He was thoughtful and miserable, and when he talked his voice was hoarse.

"Do you know what Shemayah said about me when my uncle went to ask for Avigail? Do you know what that old man said to my uncle, even though he knew that I was behind the curtain, that I could hear?"

"Jason," I said softly.

"The old man said he could see what I was from a mile away. The old man sneered. He used a Greek word for it, the word they used for Yitra and the Orphan. . . ."

"Jason, can't you see through all this?" I asked. "The man's old, bitter. When Avigail's mother died, the man died. Only Avigail keeps him breathing and walking and talking, and complaining of his sore leg."

He was beside himself. He didn't hear me.

"My uncle pretended he didn't understand him, that wicked man! My uncle, you know, he is a master of formalities. He didn't acknowledge this insult. He simply rose and said, 'Well, then perhaps you'll consider . . .' And he never even told me what Shemayah had said, that he had said—."

"Jason, Shemayah doesn't want to lose his daughter. She is all that the man has. Shemayah's the richest farmer in Nazareth and he might as well be a beggar at the foot of the hill. All he has is Avigail and he must give Avigail to someone in marriage sooner or later, and he's afraid. You come, in your fine linen and with your barbered hair, with your rings, and your gift for words in Greek and in Latin, and you make him afraid. Forgive him, Jason. Forgive him for the sake of your own heart."

He stood up. He paced.

"You don't even know what I'm talking about, do you?" he asked. "You don't understand what I'm trying to tell you!" he said. "I think one moment you understand, and the next I think you're an imbecile!"

"Jason, this place is too small for you," I said. "You wrestle with demons every day and every night in all you read, all you write, all you think, and probably in every dream you dream. Go to Jerusalem where there are men who want to talk about the world. Go to Alexandria again or Rhodes. You were happy on Rhodes. That was a good place for you, with plenty of philosophers. Maybe Rome is where you belong."

"Why should I go to any of those places?" he asked bitterly. "Why? Because you think that old man Shemayah was right?"

"No, I don't think so at all," I said.

"Well, let me tell you something, you know nothing of Rhodes or Rome or Athens, you know nothing of this world. And there comes a time when any man can be fed up with fine company, when he's tired of the taverns and the schools and the drunken banquets—when he wants to come home and walk under the trees his grandfather planted. I may not be an Essene in my heart, no, but I am a man."

"I know."

"You don't know."

"I wish I could give you what you need."

"And what is that, as if you knew!"

"My shoulder," I said. "My arms around you." I shrugged. "Kindness, that's all. I wish I could give it to you now."

He was amazed. Words boiled in him, and nothing came out of him. He turned this way and that, then back to me. "Oh, you had better not dare to do that," he whispered, staring down at me with narrow eyes. "They'd stone the both of us, if you did that, the way they stoned those boys." He moved towards the edge of the courtyard.

"In this winter," I said, "they very well might."

"You're a simpleton and a fool," he said. A whisper from the shadows.

"You know Scripture better than your uncle, don't you?" I looked at him, a dim figure now, against the lattice. Specks of light in his eyes.

"What has that to do with you and me and this?" he demanded.

"Think on it," I suggested. " 'Be kind to the stranger in your land for you were once a stranger in the land of Egypt.' " I shrugged. " 'And you know what it means to be a stranger.'. . . So tell me, how are we to treat the stranger in ourselves?"

The door of the house opened and Jason slipped back against the lattice, startled and shaken.

It was only James.

"What's the matter with *you* tonight?" he demanded of Jason. "Why are you hovering about in your linen robes? What's the matter? You look like you've lost your mind."

My heart shrank.

Jason snorted with contempt.

"Well, it's nothing a carpenter can fix," he said. "I'll tell you that much." And then he went off, up the hill.

James made some soft derisive sound. "Why do you tolerate him, why do you let him come into this courtyard and carry on as if this was a public marketplace?"

I went back to work. I said,

"You like him a lot better than you let on."

"I want to talk to you," James said.

"Not now, if you'll forgive me. I have these lines to draw. I told the others I'd do it. I sent them home."

"I know what you did," he said. "You think you are the head of this family?"

"No, James, I don't." I continued with my work.

"Now is when I choose to talk to you," he said. "Now, when the women are quiet, and the little ones are out of the way. I've come out here to talk to you, and for that reason alone."

He walked back and forth in front of the planks. I laid the planks side by side by side. Lines straight.

"James, the town's asleep. I'm almost asleep. I want to go to bed."

I drew the next line as carefully as I could. Good enough. I reached for the last plank. I stopped for a moment and rubbed my hands together. I hadn't realized it until now but my fingers were almost rigid with cold.

"Yeshua," James said in a low voice, "the time has come and you can avoid it no longer. You will marry," he said. "There is no reason any longer for you to put it off."

I looked up at him.

"I don't follow you, James."

"Don't you? Besides, where, where in all the prophecies does it say that you won't marry?" His voice was harsh. He spoke with uncommon slowness. "Whoever declared that you should not take a wife?"

I looked down again, careful to do this slowly, to move slowly so that he felt in no way more challenged than he already was.

I finished the last line. I looked over the planks. Then slowly I stood up. The pain in my knees was intense, and I bent to rub the left and then the right.

He stood with his arms folded, in a cold anger, far removed from Jason's hot currents. But in his own way, he was even angrier, and I looked past it as best I could.

"James, I will never marry," I said. "It's time we stopped this dance. It's time we put an end to it altogether. It troubles you . . . and you alone."

He put out his hand as he so often did and held my arm just tight enough for it to be painful and he didn't move.

"It does not trouble me alone," he said. "You try my patience to the limit, you do."

"I don't mean to do that," I said. "I'm tired."

"You're tired? You?" His cheeks flushed. The light of the lantern made shadows in his eyes. "The men and the women of this house have come together on it," he said. "They all say that it is time you married, and I say that you will."

"Not your father," I said. "You won't tell me that your father says so. And not my mother, because I know she would not. And if the others have come together, it's because you brought them together. And yes, I'm tired, James, and I want to go in now. I'm very tired."

I pulled loose from him as slowly as I could, and I picked up the lantern and moved towards the stable. All was done there, the beasts were fed, the place was swept and clean. Every harness was on its hook. The air was warm from the beasts. I liked it. For a moment I let it warm me.

I came back out into the yard. He had snuffed the other lantern and he stood fidgeting in the darkness and then he followed me into the house.

The family had gone to bed. Only Joseph remained by the brazier and he was asleep. His face was smooth and youthful in sleep. I loved the faces of old men; I loved their waxen purity, the way the flesh melted over their bones. I loved the distinct shapes of their eyes beneath their lids.

As I sank down by the coals and began to warm my hands, my mother came in and she stood beside James.

"Not you, too, Mother," I said.

James paced as Jason had paced. "Stubborn, proud," he said under his breath.

"No, my son," my mother said to me. "But you must know something now."

"Then tell me, Mother," I said. The warmth felt delicious to my stiffened fingers. I loved the glitter of the fire right beneath the thick gray ash of the coals.

"James, will you leave us, please?" asked my mother.

He hesitated, then he nodded respectfully, almost bowing in his respect, and he went out. Only with my mother was he that way, unfailingly gentle. He drove his wife often enough to the brink.

My mother sat down.

"This is a strange thing," she said. "You know our Avigail, and, well, you know this town is what it is, and kinsmen come asking for her from Sepphoris, even from Jerusalem."

I didn't say anything. I felt a sudden exhausting ache. I tried to locate this ache. It was in my chest, in my belly, behind my eyes. It was in my heart.

"Yeshua," my mother whispered. "The girl herself has asked for you."

Pain.

"She's far too modest to come to me with it," my mother whispered. "She's spoken to Old Bruria, and to Esther and to Salome. She's spoken to Little Salome. Yeshua, I think her father would say yes."

This pain seemed more than I could bear. I stared at the coals. I wouldn't look at my mother. I would hide this from my mother.

"My son, I know you as no one else does," said my mother. "When Avigail's with you, you're faint with love."

I couldn't answer. I couldn't command my voice. I couldn't command my heart. I remained still. Then very slowly I made my voice regular and quiet and I did speak.

"Mother," I said, "that love will go with me wherever I must go, but Avigail will not go with me. No wife will go with me—no wife, no child. Mother, you and I have never needed to talk of this. But if we must talk of it now, well then, you must know: I will not change my mind."

She nodded as I knew she would. She kissed my cheek. I held my hands out to the fire again, and she took my right hand and rubbed it with her own small warm hand.

I thought my heart would stop.

She let me go.

Avigail. This is worse than the dreams. No images to banish. Simply all I knew of her and had ever known, Avigail. This is almost more than a man can endure.

Again, I made my voice regular and small. I made it soft and without concern.

"Mother," I asked. "Was Jason really intolerable to her?"

"Jason?"

"When he asked for Avigail, Mother, was he intolerable to her? Our Jason? Do you know?"

She thought for a long moment. "My son, I don't even think Avigail ever knew that Jason asked for her," she said.

"Everyone else knew. But I think Avigail was here that day playing with the children. I'm not sure Avigail ever said a word about it. Now Shemayah came in that night, and sat here and said the most dreadful scornful things about Jason. But Avigail wasn't here then. Avigail was home, asleep. I don't know whether Avigail found Jason intolerable. No. I don't think she ever knew."

The pain had crested sometime while she was speaking. It was sharp and deep. My thoughts drifted. What a great thing it would have been to be able to cry—to be alone, and to cry, unwatched and unheard.

Flesh of my flesh and bone of my bone. I kept my face placid and my hands still. *Male and female He created them.* I had to hide this from my mother and I had to hide it from myself.

"Mother," I said, "you might mention to her—that Jason asked for her. Perhaps you can, somehow, let her know."

The pain was suddenly so bad I did not want to speak another word. I couldn't trust myself to say another word.

I felt her lips against my cheek. Her hand was on my shoulder.

After a long time, she asked, "Are you sure that's what you want me to do?"

I nodded.

"Yeshua, are you certain that it's God's will?"

I waited until the pain had backed away, and my voice would be my own again. Then I looked at her. At once her calm expression created a new calm in me.

"Mother," I said. "There are things I know, and things I don't know. Sometimes knowledge comes to me unexpectedly— in moments of surprise. Sometimes it comes when I'm pressed, and in my sudden answers to those who press me. Sometimes, this knowledge comes in pain. Always, there's the certainty that the knowledge is more than I will let myself know. It's just beyond where I choose to reach, just beyond what I choose to ask. I know it will come when I have need of it. I know it may come, as I said, on its own. But some things I know certainly and have always known. There's no surprise. There's no doubt."

She was quiet again for a while, and then she said, "This has made you miserable. I've seen this before, but never as bad as it is now."

"Is it so bad?" I whispered. I looked away, as men do when they only want to see their thoughts. "I don't know that it's been bad for me, Mother. What is bad for me? To love as I love Avigail—it has a luster, a great and beautiful luster."

She waited.

"There come these moments," I said. "These heart-breaking moments—the moments when we first feel joy and sadness intertwined. Such a discovery that is, when grief becomes sweet. I remember feeling this perhaps for the very first time when we came to this place, all of us together, and I walked up the hill above Nazareth and saw the green grass alive with flowers, the tiniest flowers—so many flowers, and all of it, grass and flowers and trees, moving as if in a great dance. It hurt."

She said nothing.

Finally I looked at her. I touched my chest with my fist lightly. "It hurt," I said. "But it was to be cherished . . . forever."

Reluctantly, she nodded.

We were both quiet.

At last I broke the silence.

"Now, tell Avigail," I said. "Let her know that Jason asked for her. Jason is devoted to her, and I must confess, life with Jason would never be dull."

She smiled. Again she kissed me, and she leaned on my shoulder as she rose to go.

James had come in. He made his pillow from his folded mantle and lay down to sleep near the wall.

I stared at the reddened coals.

"How long, O Lord?" I whispered. *How long?*

8

THE FACT WAS, all the maidens of Nazareth sighed for Jason, in their modest ways. And nowhere was it more obvious than the following evening, when the town went mad, packing into the synagogue, men and women and children alike, overflowing the benches, huddling in the doorway, and crowded together on the floor right up to the feet of the Rabbi and the elders.

At the first darkening, the signal fires had flashed the news into Galilee, which had already spread throughout Judea. Pontius Pilate's men had indeed installed their ensigns within the Holy City, and refused over the protests of the angry populace to remove them.

Blast after blast came from the ram's horn.

Pushed and shoved, we took our places as close to Joseph as we could, James struggling to control his sons, Menachim, Isaac, and Shabi. All my nephews were there, my cousins—in fact, every able-bodied man in Nazareth, it seemed, and those who couldn't walk on their own were being carried in on the shoulders of their sons or grandsons. Old Sherebiah who could no longer hear was being carried in.

Avigail, Silent Hannah, and my aunts were already seated among the agitated but largely silent women.

As Jason moved forward to declare the news in full, I saw Avigail's eyes fixed on him with the same absorption as the others.

Jason climbed up and stood on the bench beside the seated elders.

How dazzling he was in his daily white linen and blue tassels, with a bleached mantle over his shoulders. No teacher under Solomon's Porch ever looked more commanding, or ever so elegant.

"How many years ago was it," cried Jason, "that Tiberius Caesar expelled the entire Jewish community from Rome?"

A roar went up from the assembly, even the women crying out, but all fell silent as Jason went on: "And now as we all know, this equestrian, Sejanus, rules the world for this heartless Emperor, whose own son, Drusus, Sejanus murdered!"

The Rabbi rose at once, demanding silence. We were all shaking our heads. This was a dangerous thing to say even in the farthest corner of the Empire. Never mind that everyone believed it. The ancient elders clamored as well for Jason to be still. Joseph motioned sternly for him to be silent.

"Reports of these ensigns in the Holy City have already gone to Tiberius Caesar," cried the Rabbi. "Surely they have. You think the Lord High Priest Joseph Caiaphas stands by and watches this blasphemy in silence? You think Herod Antipas is doing nothing? And you know full well, every one of you, that this Emperor wants no riots in these parts, or anywhere in the Empire. The Emperor will send an order as he has done in the past. The ensigns will be removed. Pontius Pilate will have no choice in it!"

Joseph and the elders vigorously gave their agreement. The eyes of the younger men and women were fixed on Jason. And Jason only watched, unsatisfied. Then Jason shook his head No.

Again came the murmuring and suddenly shouts as well.

"Patience is what is required of us now," Joseph said, and some attempted to hush others so that he could be heard. He was the only one of the elders even attempting to speak. But it was useless.

Then Jason's voice rang out sharp and mocking, above the noise.

"What if the Emperor himself never sees such a report?" demanded Jason. "What assurance do we have that this Sejanus, who despises our race, and always has, won't intercept the report? And the Emperor will never lay eyes on it?"

Louder came the cries of agreement.

Menachim, James' eldest, rose to his feet. "I say we march on Caesarea, all of us, that we go in a body, demanding that the Governor take the ensigns out of the city."

Jason's eyes blazed and he drew Menachim towards him.

"I forbid you to go!" James shouted, and other men his age cried out with equal force, attempting to stop the young men who seemed on the verge of running out of the assembly.

My uncle Cleopas stood up. He bellowed: "Silence, you mad rabble."

He took a stand beside the elders.

"What do any of you know?" he said, pointing his finger at Menachim and Shabi and Jason and a host of others as he turned this way and that. "Tell me, what do you know of the Roman legions marching down into this land from Syria? What in your miserable little lifetimes have you seen of this? You hotheaded children!" He glared at Jason.

Then he climbed up on the bench, not even reaching for a hand to help him, and he forced Jason to the side, and nearly toppled him.

Cleopas was no elder. He was not as old as the youngest of the elders, who was, in fact, his brother-in-law Joseph. But

Cleopas had a full head of gray hair framing his vigorous face, and he had a powerful voice with the timbre of youth and the authority of a teacher.

"Answer me," Cleopas demanded. "How many times, Menachim bar James, have you seen Roman soldiers in Galilee? Well, who has seen them, you, you . . . you?"

"Tell them," declared the Rabbi to Cleopas, "because they don't know. And those who do know apparently cannot remember."

The younger men went into a rage, shouting that they knew full well what they meant to do, or what they had to do, and began trying to outdo one another in volume.

Cleopas raised his voice louder than I'd ever heard it. He gave them all a taste of the oratory we were used to under our own roof.

"You don't think this Sejanus, whom you so detest," he declared, "will not move to stop riots in Judea? The man doesn't want riots. He wants power, and he wants it in Rome, and he wants no noise from the eastern Empire. I say let him have his power. The Jews have long been back in Rome. The Jews are at peace in every city of the world from Rome to Babylon. And what do you know of how this peace was forged, you who would run headlong into the Roman guard at Caesarea?"

"We know we are Jews, that's what we know," declared Menachim. James wanted to strike him, but held back.

Across the way, my mother shut her eyes and bowed her head. Avigail stared wide eyed at Jason, who stood with his arms folded as if he were the judge of the matter, eyeing the small gathering of the elders coldly.

"What history are you going to tell us?" Jason demanded, looking at Cleopas as the two stood side by side. "Are you going to tell us that we had decades of peace under Augustus?

We know that. Are you going to tell us we've had peace under Tiberius? We know that. Are you going to tell us the Romans tolerate our laws? We know that. But we know the ensigns, the ensigns with the figure of Tiberius, are in the Holy City now and that they've been there since morning. And we know that the High Priest Joseph Caiaphas has not had them removed. Nor has Herod Antipas. Why? Why have they not been removed? I'll tell you why. Force is the only voice this new Governor, Pontius Pilate, will understand. He was sent here by a brutal man, and he is in league with a brutal man, and who among us did not know that this could happen!"

The cry that went up was deafening. The building was beating with it like a great drum. Even the women were inflamed. Avigail huddled close to my mother, staring at Jason with amazement. Even Silent Hannah, her eyes still dull with pain, regarded him with vague wonder.

"Silence!" cried Cleopas. He roared the word again and stamped on the bench until the noise died down. "That is not so, what you say, and what is it to us, what the man is? We are not brutal men." He beat on his breast with both hands. "Force is not our language! It may be the language of this foolish Governor and his cronies, but we speak with a different tongue and we always have. If you don't think the legions can come down out of Syria and fill this land with crosses in a month then you know nothing. Look at your fathers. Look at your grandfathers! Are you more zealous for the law than they are?" He pointed here and here and there. He pointed to James. He pointed to me. He pointed to Joseph.

"We remember the year when Herod Archaelaus was deposed," Cleopas said. "Ten years the man ruled, and then he was made to step down. And what happened in the land when the Emperor, on our behalf, took this action? I'll tell you what happened. Judas the Galilean and his Pharisee con-spirator rose up, out of those mountains, and filled the coun-tryside in Judea and Galilee and Samaria with murder and fire and pillage and riot! And we who'd seen it before, this very carnage at the death of Old Herod, we saw it again, in wave after wave, like a blaze in a dead field licking the grass out of the very air with tongues of flame. And down the Romans came as they always do, and the crosses went up and to walk those roads out there was to walk amid the cries and the groans of the dying."

Silence. Even Jason gazed at Cleopas in silence.

"Now will you bring that here again?" asked Cleopas. "You will not. You will stay where you are, in this village, here, in Nazareth, and you will let the High Priest and his advisors write to Caesar and lay before him this blasphemy! You will let those men set sail, as surely they will. And you will await their decision."

For one moment, it seemed the battle was won. Then a cry rose from the doorway. "But everyone's going; they're all going . . . to Caesarea."

Protests and fierce declarations rose on all sides.

Jason shook his head. The older men were rising to their feet, pushing and arguing, and men reached for their sons.

Menachim pulled back from James, defying him, and James blushed red with anger.

"Men are on their way now," cried another voice from the back. And yet another. "A crowd is halfway there from Jerusalem!"

Jason shouted above the melee. "These things are true," he said. "Men won't bear this insolence, this blasphemy, in silence. If Joseph Caiaphas thinks we will bear it to keep the peace, then he is wrong! I say we go to Caesarea, with our countrymen!" Shouts and screams rose louder and louder, but he was not finished. "I say we go not to riot, no! That would be folly. Cleopas is right. We go not to fight, but to stand before this man, this arrogant man, and tell him he has breached our laws and we will not stand down until he acknowledges us!"

Pandemonium. No young man was left on the floor; all stood, some jumping in their excitement, like the children who were pumping their fists furiously and leaping this way and that. Most of the women had risen. And others had to rise, as they couldn't see over the others. The benches from one end of the room rattled and thumped with the dancing feet.

Menachim and Isaac pushed their way to Jason's side and took their stand with him, glaring up at their uncle. Menachim took ahold of Jason's mantle. All the young men struggled towards Jason.

James grabbed for Menachim's arm, and before his son could get away, James gave him the back of his hand hard, but Menachim stood firm.

"Stop this now, all of you," James cried out, but in vain.

A gasp came from Joseph. I felt it, though I couldn't hear it.

"You go into Caesarea as a body," cried Cleopas, "and the Romans will draw their swords. You think they care whether you carry daggers or plowshares!"

The Rabbi echoed these words. The elders struggled to add their agreement, but it was all lost in the passionate cries of the young.

Menachim climbed up onto the bench beside Jason, and Cleopas, thrown off balance, fell. I caught him so that he stood on the ground on his feet.

"We go," cried Jason, "we go together to stand before Pontius Pilate in such numbers he cannot imagine. What is

Nazareth to be, a byword for cowardice! Who is a Jew that won't go with us?"

A new wave of noise swept over us, shaking the very walls again, and for the first time, I heard the volume of cries outside the synagogue. People outside were beating on the walls. The night was filled with cries. I could hear them behind us.

Suddenly the crowd at the door was broken open by a band of men, clothed for the road, with their wineskins over their shoulders. Two I knew from Cana, one from Sepphoris.

"We go to Caesarea, tonight. We go to stand before the Governor's palace until he removes the ensigns!" cried one of the men.

Joseph gestured for me to help him. He reached for Cleopas. We managed to get him up on the bench. Menachim stepped down to make way for him, and even Jason stepped aside, as well he might.

Joseph stood for a moment staring at the maddened crowd. He threw up his hands. The noise rolled on like a flood that would drown him, but slowly it began to subside, and then at the sight of this white-haired man, saying nothing, merely gesturing with both arms raised as if he meant to part the Red Sea, they all fell quiet.

"Very well then, my children," he said. Even the smallest murmurs died away. "You must learn for yourselves what we know so well, we who saw Judas the Galilean and his men running rampant through these hills, we who have seen the legions more than once come into this land to restore order. Yes, yes. Very well, then. You learn for yourselves what you won't learn from us."

James went to protest. He held tight to Isaac who struggled against him.

"No, my son," said Joseph to James. "Don't put temptation before them. You forbid this, and they will do it anyway."

At that a soft respecting applause filled the room. Then murmurs and finally roars of approbation.

Joseph went on, arms still raised.

"Show the Governor your fervor, yes. Jason, show your eloquence, if you will, yes. Speak to this man in your perfect Latin, yes. But walk and talk in peace, do you hear me? I tell you once the glittering swords of the Romans are unsheathed, they will cut down all of us. A Roman army will make the way straight to this village."

Jason turned to face him and then clutched Joseph's right hand as if they were in agreement.

"As the Lord lives," Jason cried out. "They will take down those ensigns or drink our blood. It's their decision."

One voice of wild accord rose to answer him.

Jason jumped down from the bench and marched forward, pushing everyone out of his path, and soon the whole assembly was trying to get out of the door and into the street to follow him.

Benches rattled and clattered and babies sobbed.

The Rabbi sat down wearily and leant his head against my shoulder. My nephews Shabi and Isaac escaped from James' hands and squeezed past others to run after their brother Menachim.

I thought James would go mad.

Jason turned in the door, reemerging from the angry sea of those around him. He looked back as all streamed past him.

"And will you not come with us, you above all?" he demanded. He flung out his pointing finger.

"No," I said. I shook my head and looked away.

The sound of my answer hadn't carried in the din, but

the shape of it did, and he was gone and all the younger men with him.

The street was so full of torches it might as well have been the night of the Exodus from Egypt. Men were now laughing and hollering as they dodged in and out of their houses to get their heavy woolen robes and wineskins for the trek.

James caught his young son, Isaac, and when Isaac, a boy of no more than ten, struggled, Avigail suddenly seized him and demanded fiercely, "What, would you leave me here alone? Do you think no one has to take care of this village?"

She held fast to him in a way that his father could never have done, because Isaac wouldn't fight her. And she rallied to herself the other young boys, all that she could see. "You come here, Yaqim, and you too, Little Levi. And you, Benjamin!" Silent Hannah took up the exhortations.

Of course other women, young and old, were doing the same, each dragging out of the march any whom they could handle.

And into the village came more men from the countryside, farmhands, men of the villages near and far that everyone knew, and I saw finally even the soldiers, Herod's soldiers from Sepphoris.

"Are you with us?" someone shouted.

I covered my ears.

I walked on into the house.

Avigail all but dragged Isaac in with her. James was too angry to look at him. Menachim and Shabi were already on their way out as we entered, and Menachim looked once at James as if he would cry, but then he said, "Father, I have to go!" and off he went as James turned his back, and let his head sink on his chest.

Little Isaac began to cry. "My brothers, I have to go with them, Avigail."

"You will not," Avigail said. She reached for her ducklings. "I tell you, you will stay here with me." She held six or seven of them in thrall.

My mother helped Joseph to be seated near the fire.

"How can this all begin again?" asked Cleopas. "And where is Silas!" he suddenly demanded. "Where is Little Joseph?" He looked around in panic. "Where are my sons!" he roared.

"They're gone," said Avigail. "They came to the assembly ready to go." She shook her head at the pity of it. She held Isaac by his wrist, though he struggled.

Avigail's father, Shemayah, came into the room, hulking, breathless, out of sorts—he saw Avigail with her children, and making a disgusted gesture walked out and home before anyone could offer him a cup of wine or water.

Avigail sat amongst the boys, most of them ten or eleven years old, and one, Yaqim, who was twelve. She held fast to Yaqim's hand just as she held Isaac's hand. Yaqim had no mother, and in all likelihood his father was drunk in the tavern.

"I need you all here, we need you," Avigail maintained, "and I won't hear another word on it. None of you go. You stay here tonight under this roof, where Yeshua and James can watch you. And you girls, you come with me, tonight, and you." She tugged at Silent Hannah.

Suddenly she paused, and she came to me.

"Yeshua," she said. "What do you think *will* happen?"

I looked up at her. How tender and curious she seemed, how far from any real dread.

"Will Jason speak for them?" she asked. "Will he put the case before the Governor for them?"

"My dearest child," I said, "there are a thousand Jasons now making their way to Caesarea. There are priests and scribes and scholars on their way."

"And brigands," said Cleopas, disgusted. "Brigands who'll mix with the crowd, who'll bring the whole thing to riot at a moment's notice if they think they'll have the fight they've always wanted, the fight they never wanted to give up, the fight they still maintain in every backcountry cave and tavern."

Avigail was suddenly afraid, as were all the women, until James urged Cleopas to please leave off, and Joseph said the same.

Old Bruria came into the room, the eldest of our household, a woman not related to us by blood but one who'd lived with us from long ago when the land had run with blood after the death of Old Herod.

"Enough," said Bruria in a dark, strong voice. "Pray, Avigail, pray as we all pray. The teachers of the Temple are on the road. They were on the road before the signal fires even glittered on the evening mountains." She stood beside Joseph. She waited.

She wanted Joseph to lead us in prayer, but he seemed to have forgotten. His brother Alphaeus came into the room, and only then did any of us think that he had not even come to the assembly. He sat down beside his brother.

"Very well, then," said Bruria. "O Lord, Maker of the Universe, have mercy on Your people Israel."

All night long the village was alive with the sounds of men passing through on their way south.

Sometimes when I could no longer sleep, I went out in the courtyard and as I stood there, hugging my arms in the dark, I could hear the raucous voices from the tavern.

At dawn, riders came to the village, reading aloud their

brief letters, declaring that this or that town had sent all its occupants south to appeal to the Governor.

Some of the older men put on their robes and got their walking sticks and set out to join those marching through.

Even some of the old men, on their donkeys, wrapped in blankets to their noses, made their way.

James worked without a word, banging the hammer with more strength than needed for the slightest nail.

Mary, the wife of Little Cleopas, broke into sobs. Not only had he gone on, but so had her father, Levi, and her brothers. And word had come that every man worth his salt was joining the movement to Caesarea.

"Well, not this man worth his salt," said James. He threw the lumber into the cart. "There's no point to going to work," he said. "This can wait. Everything can wait, as we wait on the windows of Heaven."

The sky was a pale soiled blue. And the wind was filled with the smells of the unwashed stables and courtyards, of the dying fields, of the urine drawing flies to the stained plaster.

The next night was quiet. They were all gone. What could the signal fires say except that more and more people were taking to the roads, except that they came from the north and the south and the east and the west? And that the ensigns remained in the Holy City.

James said to me at dawn:

"I used to think you would change things."

"Remember yourself," said my mother. She set down the bread and olives for us. She poured the water.

"I did," said James, glaring at me. "I used to think you would change it all. I used to believe in what I'd seen with my two eyes—the gifts of the Magi laid down in the straw, the faces of shepherds who'd heard angels fill up the sky. I used to believe that."

"James, I beg you," said my mother.

"Let him alone," said Joseph softly. "James has said these words many a time. So we bear with him again."

"And you, Father," James asked. "Have you never thought, what was the meaning of all of it?"

"The Lord made Time," said Joseph. "And the Lord will reveal all in Time when He wants to reveal it."

"And my sons will die," said James. His face was twisted with anguish. "My sons will die the way men died before, and for what?"

Avigail came in with Silent Hannah, and the usual following of little ones.

"Please no more talk of this," said my aunt Esther.

"My father says the world has gone to Caesarea," said Avigail. "We had a letter from our cousins in Bethany. Your cousins, our cousins, all of them from Bethany. They've gone as well." She burst into tears.

All the children crowded around her to comfort her. "They'll all come home," said Isaac, her little protector. He snuggled up to her immediately. "I promise you, Avigail. I give you my word. They'll be back. My brothers will be back. Stop. You'll make Silent Hannah cry. . . ."

"And who is left in Nazareth, do you think?" asked James bitterly. He turned to me. "Ah!" he said with mock surprise. "Yeshua, the Sinless."

Avigail looked up, startled. Her eyes moved over the faces of everyone there. She looked at me.

"And James, the Just! Is left here too," declared my aunt Esther.

"James, the Merciless!" said Aunt Salome. "Be quiet, or go yourself."

"No, no . . . hush now, all of you," said my mother.

"Yes, please, I didn't mean to . . . I'm sorry," said Avigail.

"You did nothing," I said.

And so on the day went.

And the next day.

And the day after.

9

THE BRIGANDS HIT THE VILLAGE AT DAWN.

James and I had just come out of the Rabbi's door. We stood at the top of the hill. And we saw them—two ragged men on horseback—racing down the far slope towards the creek.

The women with their water jars and bundles of laundry screamed and scattered in all directions, children racing with them.

James and I gave the alarm. The horn was blasting as we ran towards the men.

Only one drove his mount uphill right towards us, and as people came out of the doors on all sides, he pressed into us and we fell backwards, the hooves stomping past our heads.

"Avigail," James cried out. "Avigail" came another shout and then another. As I scrambled to my feet, my hand bleeding, I saw what all saw: the man who stayed behind had snatched her up by the waist. The children hurled their stones at him. Isaac dragged at the man's left shoulder.

Avigail screamed and kicked. The children grabbed hold of her flailing ankles.

All the women rushed at the man, hurling their jars at his horse.

We reached the creek bed as, assailed on all sides, the ruffian let loose of Avigail, pulling her veil and mantle free as she slammed to the rocky ground. Brandishing her robes like a flag the man, ducking low to escape the hail of stones flung at him, rode away as fast as he could.

Avigail scrambled up, drawing her knees under her and bending forward. She was in her long-sleeved tunic and her hair was streaming over her face and shoulders. Little Isaac threw his arms around her to shield her from all eyes.

I reached her and went down on my knees in front of her and took her by the shoulders.

She screamed my name and clung to me. Blood ran from her forehead and her cheek.

"They're gone," cried James. All the women surrounded us. My aunt Esther cried she'd gotten the man good with her jar. She'd broken it on his very head. The children were sobbing and running to and fro.

Cries came from above.

"The other one's gone. He was the distraction," declared James. "They wanted a woman, the godless heathens, will you look at this, look what they've done."

"It's over," I whispered to Avigail. "Let me look at you. These are scratches and scrapes."

She nodded. She understood me.

Then I heard a voice over my head.

"Stand back from my daughter. Get your hands off her."

I could scarce believe these words were meant for me.

My aunt Esther gestured for me to draw back. She took her place by Avigail as Avigail climbed to her feet.

"She's unharmed," said Aunt Esther. "We were all here and we gave him rocks and stones and blows for his pains, I can tell you."

There was a chorus of agreement.

Shemayah stared at Avigail as she stood there, shivering, in her long wool tunic, her hair disheveled, the cuts bleeding on her face.

I took off my mantle and quickly put it over her shoulders. But he thrust me back and off balance as she took it. The women hastily put it over her. Her tunic was modest enough. It was plenty enough. But now she was fully draped as usual in a mantle over her shoulders and down her back. And my aunt Salome drew back Avigail's loose hair.

Shemayah picked up his daughter. He picked her up in both arms as if she were a child and carried her up the hill.

The women ran after him, and the children, crowding and hampering his every step.

James and I waited. Then slowly we climbed the hill.

When we reached his door, the women stood outside staring at the wood.

"What is this? Why haven't you gone in?" I demanded.

"He won't let us go in."

My mother came out of our house with Old Bruria. "What's happened?"

Everyone told a version of it at once.

Old Bruria pounded on the door. "Shemayah," she cried. "You open this door now for us. This girl needs us."

The door opened, and out came Silent Hannah flung at us as if she were no more than a bundle of clothes.

The door slammed shut.

Silent Hannah was terrified.

I knocked on the door. I put my voice close to the wood, gesturing for James to stay back and not try to stop me.

"Shemayah," I called out. "The women are here to tend to Avigail, let them in."

"She was not hurt!" declared my aunt Salome. "We all saw it. She fought, and he dropped her! You all saw it."

"Yes, we all saw it," said Aunt Esther. "All of you men go, leave here, you leave this to us."

We backed up as they told us to do. More women had come. James' wife, Mara, and Mary of Little Cleopas and Silas' wife and at least a dozen more. The older women pounded all together on the door.

"Force it!" said Esther, and they flung themselves at the door, kicking and pounding, until it rocked free of its pivots and fell in.

I moved to where I could see into the dimly lighted room. I caught only a glimpse before it was filled with women. Avigail, white and crying, disheveled as before, like a bundle flung in the corner, the blood still dripping from her head.

The roaring protests of Shemayah were drowned out by the women. Isaac and Yaqim and Silent Hannah tried to get into the house but they couldn't get in. It was too filled with the women.

And it was the women who put the door back up on its pivots and closed it against us.

We went into our own courtyard, and James let go with words.

"Is he mad?" I demanded.

"Don't be such a fool," said my uncle Cleopas. "The bandit ripped off her veil."

"What is her veil?" demanded James. Isaac and Yaqim came to us crying. "What in the name of the Lord does it matter that he took her veil?"

"He's an old and stupid man," said Cleopas. "I don't defend him. I'm only answering you because it seems someone has to answer you."

"We saved her," Isaac said to his father, wiping at his tears.

James kissed his son's head and held him close. "You did well, all of you," he said. "Yaqim, you, and you," he pointed to the little boys who hovered in the street. "Come inside now."

It was a full hour before my mother came in with Aunt Esther and Aunt Salome.

Aunt Salome was furious.

"He's sent for the midwife."

"How can he do such a thing!" cried James. "The whole village saw this. Nothing happened. The man was forced to let her go."

My mother sat crying by the brazier.

There was shouting from the street, mostly the voices of women. Yaqim and Isaac ran out before anyone could stop them.

I didn't move.

Finally Old Bruria came in. "The midwife has come and gone," she said. "Let it be known to all this house and every house, and every lout and bully and no-count in this village who wants to know it, and fret about it, and gossip about it, the girl is unharmed."

"Well, that's hardly a surprise," said Aunt Esther. "And you left her alone with him?"

Old Bruria made a gesture as if to say she could do no more, and she went off to her room.

Silent Hannah who had seen everything got up quietly and slipped out the door.

I wanted to follow. I wanted to see whether or not Shemayah would let her in. But I didn't do this. Only my mother followed and came back moments later and nodded and so it was over for now.

At noon, Shemayah and his field hands rode out into the hills. Inside his house, his two maidservants remained with

Avigail and with Silent Hannah, bolting the door behind him as he told them to do.

We knew he wouldn't find the bandits. We prayed he wouldn't find the bandits. He didn't know what to do against men armed with daggers and swords. And the ragged bunch he'd taken with him were only the older men and the weaker men, the men who hadn't gone off to Caesarea to take a stand.

Sometime during the early evening, Shemayah returned. We heard the noise of the horses, not a common sound in our street.

My mother and aunts went to his door and begged to see Avigail. He wouldn't answer.

All the next day no one came or went from the house of Shemayah. His field hands gathered, then wandered off without directions.

It was the same the following day.

Meanwhile, news came in every few hours from Caesarea.

And on the third day after the attack of the bandits, we had a long letter in Jason's hand, read out in the synagogue, that the crowd was peaceably assembled before the Governor's palace and would not be moved.

This gave comfort to the Rabbi and comfort to many of the rest of us. Though some simply wondered what the Governor would do if this crowd did not go away.

Neither Shemayah nor anyone from his house came to the assembly.

The next day, Shemayah went out to his fields at dawn. No one answered when the women knocked. Then Silent Hannah came out quietly in the afternoon.

She came into our house and told the women in gestures that Avigail lay on the floor. That Avigail took nothing to eat. That Avigail took nothing to drink. In a little while, she hurried back, fearful that Shemayah might have returned and found her gone, and she disappeared into the house and the bolt was again in place.

I didn't find these things out until I'd returned from work in Sepphoris. My mother told me what Silent Hannah had let them know.

The house was miserable.

Joseph and Bruria went together and knocked. They were truly our eldest, the ones no one should refuse. But Shemayah didn't answer them. And slowly Bruria helped Joseph back into the house.

10

THE NEXT MORNING we went to the Rabbi, all of us together, the women who'd been there at the creek, the children who'd been there, and James and I and others who'd seen it. Old Bruria came with us, and so did Joseph though it seemed harder than ever for him to make the journey up the hill. We asked for a meeting with the Rabbi and we all went to the synagogue together, and we closed the doors.

It was clean and quiet there. The morning sun had even made it a little warm. Joseph was seated on the bench. The Rabbi took his usual place in his chair to Joseph's right.

"It comes to this," I said, standing before the Rabbi. "Avigail, our kinswoman, was not harmed by this man. All here saw what happened; they saw her fight; they saw her relinquished. They saw her taken home. Now days have passed. Silent Hannah comes and goes but only Silent Hannah, and Silent Hannah says, as best she can, that Avigail neither eats nor drinks."

The Rabbi nodded. His shoulders were hunched under his robes. His eyes were filled with pity.

"Now we ask only this," I said, "that her cousins here, these women, be allowed to attend to her, to the cuts and scrapes she received when she was thrown to the ground. We ask that they be allowed to go in to her. To see that she takes what food and drink she should. Her father won't allow it. The servants are doddering old women. It was Avigail who cared for these servants. How can these servants now care for Avigail? Surely Avigail is frightened and crying, and suffering alone."

"I know all this," said the Rabbi sadly. "You know I know. And her father went off after the evildoers. He went riding out to soak his rusty sword in blood. And he wasn't the only one. They struck Cana, those bandits. No, they didn't steal a woman, just everything else they could grab. The King's soldiers will catch them. They've sent a cohort into the hills."

"Be that as it may," I said. "Our concern is for our kinswoman Avigail."

"Rabbi, you must make him let us in," said Old Bruria. "The girl needs tending. She might be losing her wits."

"And worse, there's talk in the village," said Aunt Esther.

"What talk?" James asked. "What are you saying?"

My aunts were exasperated at James, but my mother was merely shocked.

"If I didn't have to go to the market again, I wouldn't," said Aunt Esther. Mara, James' wife, nodded, and said that she would not either were it her choice.

"What are they saying?" asked the Rabbi wearily. "What talk?"

"Everything imaginable," said Aunt Esther, "and what on earth do you expect? They're saying that she was dawdling, that she was singing to the children, that she was dancing as she likes to do. That she was drawing attention to herself. Beautiful Avigail, Avigail the one with the lovely voice. That she was away from the others. That she had taken off her veil to show off her hair. On and on and on. Have I forgotten anything? None of it, not a word of it, not a single word, is true! We were there and we saw it. She is the youngest, the prettiest, of that she's guilty, and whose fault is that?"

I walked over to the bench and sat down, not far from Joseph. And I put my elbows on my knees. I had suspected as much but I hated to hear it. I was tempted to put my hands over my ears.

My mother spoke up softly. "Shemaya invites shame on himself with this way of behaving," she said. "Rabbi, please, go with Old Bruria and talk to him, and let the girl have company, and let her come to us as before."

"To you?" asked the Rabbi. "You think he will let her come to you?"

All stared at him in silence. I sat up and looked at him.

He was as sad as before, with a faraway look in his eye as he pondered.

"And why not to us?" asked Aunt Esther.

"Yeshua," said the Rabbi. He pulled himself up and looked at me, but his eyes were gentle. "What did you do at the creek? What was it that you did?"

"Why, what are you asking him!" James said. "He did nothing. He went to help her as a brother would help her!"

Aunt Esther broke in, "She was lying on the rough ground where the cutthroat had thrown her. She was bleeding. She was terrified. He went to her to help her to her feet. He gave her his mantle."

"Ah," said the Rabbi.

"Someone says different?" demanded James.

"Who is talking about this?" demanded Aunt Esther.

"You have some doubt on this matter!" asked Bruria. "Lord Jacimus, surely you don't think—."

"None," said the Rabbi. "I have no doubt. So you helped her to her feet and you gave her your mantle."

"I did," I answered.

"Well, then!" said Bruria.

"Let us take things one at a time," said the Rabbi. "What good is it for a Pharisee to go talk to this man who has in his mind no use for Pharisees, no use for Essenes, no use for anyone or anything except old farmers like himself who bury their gold in the ground? What good is it for me to go to his door?"

"And so what, this poor child is now walled up alive in that house with this angry man who can't string three words together except when driven by rage?" demanded Bruria.

"Wait, that's what you have to do," said the Rabbi. "Wait."

"The girl should be seen now," said Bruria. "She should be attended, and she should come out of the house and visit with her kinsmen, and she should tell the tale in a soft voice to those nearest her, and she should go to the stream again, accompanied by her kindred, and she should go in and go out! What does it say that she is locked up as if she's not to be seen!"

"I know this, Bruria," said the Rabbi somberly. "And you are her kindred."

"How many witnesses does this require!" demanded Uncle Cleopas. "This girl's done nothing. Nothing's happened to her, except that someone tried to harm her, and that one was stopped."

"The witnesses were all women and children," said the Rabbi.

"No, they were not!" declared James. "My brother and I saw all of it. My brother—." He stopped, staring at me.

I looked up at him. It wasn't necessary for me to say anything. He understood.

"No, say whatever it is," said Bruria, looking from me to James and to the Rabbi. "Say this aloud."

"Yeshua," said the Rabbi, "if only you hadn't gone to the girl and embraced her."

"Good Lord, Rabbi," said James. "He did what was natural. He did what was kind."

My mother shook her head. "We're the same family," she whispered.

"I know all this. But this man, Shemayah, is not one of your family; his wife was, yes, and Avigail is, yes. But this man is not. And this man does not have a subtle mind."

"I don't understand it, truly I don't," said James. "Have patience with me. Are you telling me this man thinks my brother hurt Avigail?"

"No, only that he took liberties with her. . . ."

"Took liberties!" cried James.

"These are not my thoughts," said the Rabbi. "I am only telling you why the man will not let you in, and as you are her kindred, and her only kindred in Nazareth, I say wait because waiting for him to change his mind is all that you can do."

"What of her kindred elsewhere?" asked Bruria.

"Ah, well," said the Rabbi, "what are we to do, to write to her kindred in Bethany? To the house of Joseph Caiaphas? It would take days for the letter to get there, and the High Priest and his family have more on their minds than the goings-on in this town, must I remind you of that? Besides, what is it you think your kindred in Bethany can do?"

They went on talking, softly, reasonably. Joseph sat with his eyes closed as if he slept. Bruria went about this as if it were a knot that she could loosen if she were patient enough.

I heard their voices but their words didn't penetrate. I sat alone, staring at the sunlight as it cut into the dust, and thinking only this: I had hurt Avigail. I had added to her woes. At a time of violence and disgrace, I'd added to her burdens. I'd done this. And this could not stand.

Finally I made a motion for silence. I stood up.

"Yes, what is it, Yeshua," said the Rabbi.

"You know I will lay my apologies before the man," I said, "but he would never allow me to say such things."

"This is true."

"I would go with my father and my father would beg him," I said, "but the man would never allow us to come in the door."

"This is true."

"Well, then, you spoke of kindred. You spoke of kindred elsewhere."

"I did."

"On her mother's side, our side, we have cousins in Sepphoris. But more to the point, we have cousins in Cana, whom you know very well. Hananel of Cana is your old friend. He's the first who comes to mind, but there are others. However, Hananel is a well-spoken and persuasive man."

Everyone nodded to this. We all knew Hananel.

I went on to the Rabbi,

"We laid the marble floors of his house years ago," I said. "On many a pilgrimage, I've spoken with Hananel, all the way to the festival, as have you."

"Yes, yes, and the very last time," said the Rabbi, "as we all went together, Hananel called my nephew Jason a nuisance and a curse, am I not correct?"

"I don't speak in connection with Jason, Rabbi," I said. "I speak in connection with Avigail. The old man is surely at home. We would have heard if he had left Cana to go to Caesarea, and we have not. He knows all of the family of Avigail's mother, and he's closer in kinship to her than he is to us."

"That's true," said James, "but he's an old man living alone with no sons living and his grandson is roaming the world, only Heaven knows where. What can he do?"

"He can come and talk to Shemayah and reason this matter out with him," I said. "And he can write to the kindred we don't know far and wide and he can find a place for Avigail to lodge. She need not starve to death in this village. This is not to be borne. She can go to her people in Sepphoris or in Capernaum or in Jerusalem. Hananel will know them. Hananel is a scholar and a Scribe and a judge. Hananel can speak where we can't be heard."

"This is possible. . . ." murmured the Rabbi.

"I'll go to him," I said. "I'll explain what happened. I'll lay before him the whole story as I saw it, and my own clumsiness. And he will understand."

"Yeshua, you are as brave as Daniel, to put your head in the lion's mouth," said the Rabbi, "however . . ."

"I'll go to him. It won't take an hour for me to get to Cana. What can he do? Turn me down."

"He has a mean tongue, Yeshua. He makes Shemayah look like a flower of the field for cheerfulness and sweetness. He does nothing but bemoan his wandering grandson, and he blames Jason for it. Jason. He blames Jason that his grandson is under a porch in Athens disputing with the heathens."

"It's no matter to me, Rabbi," I said. "He can heap me with insults. He has a clever tongue and a relentless tongue, and no patience for men like Shemayah. And I think he will remember his cousin Avigail, above all."

Joseph lifted his hand.

"I *know* he will remember his cousin Avigail," Joseph said softly. "We old ones," he said. He paused as if he'd lost his thought and then went on with vague eyes. "We watch the young ones on the pilgrimage, as if they were flocks of birds we must keep to the road. I've seen him many a time smiling at Avigail. When the girls broke into singing, he listened to Avigail. I saw him. And one time, over a cup of wine in the Temple Court as we sat together on the last day of the festival, he told me he heard her voice in his sleep. That wasn't so long ago. Perhaps two years ago. Who knows?"

This was exactly what I'd seen as well.

"I'll go then," I said. "I'll ask him to find a household for Avigail, away from Nazareth, where she can be properly cared for, and where she can rest."

Joseph looked up at me.

"Be careful, my son," he said. "He will be kind to Avigail, but not to you."

"He will bait you," said the Rabbi, "try to rattle you with his arguments and draw you in with his questions. He has nothing else to do in his library. And he is sick over the loss of his grandson, though he himself drove the boy away."

"So give me some armor for this journey, my lord?" I suggested.

"You'll know what to say," said the Rabbi. "Explain it as you have here. And don't let him drive you out of the house. If I were to go with you, we'd be in a battle, he and I, at once."

"Ask that he write to the family which is best for her," said Joseph. "And when such arrangements are made, that there is a place for her, let him come. Let him come and the Rabbi and I will go with him to see Shemayah."

"Yes," said the Rabbi. "The man can't turn away Hananel."

"Hananel! He's the son of insults," said James under his breath. "He once told me while I was working on his very walls that he would move Cana stone by stone so that it was farther away from Nazareth if only he could do so."

The Rabbi laughed.

"Perhaps he'll be proud to rescue the beloved child from this miserable place," Bruria offered.

Joseph smiled and winked and pointed agreeably at Bruria. He looked at me and whispered,

"Such is the path, perhaps, to the man's heart."

I took my leave, letting them come behind me. For this I needed a pair of better sandals, and fresh clothes. It wasn't a long walk, but the wind was fierce.

After I was dressed and ready to go, my mother drew me aside, though my brothers, as they prepared for work, were all watching her.

"Listen, what you did by the creek," she said. "It was kind, don't you ever think that it wasn't."

I nodded.

"It's just, well, you see, Avigail had asked her father . . . as well as us. She'd asked Shemayah if he would look kindly on you. It was before she spoke to us and before we told her that such a thing wouldn't happen."

"I see," I said.

"Have I wounded you?"

"No. I understand. He's been doubly shamed."

"Yes, and not a wise man, and not a patient one."

And what of her, my Avigail? What of her at this very moment when the sun beat down on the noisy town. In what dark room was she locked away, staring into the shadows?

I took a walking stick for good company and headed out for Cana.

11

THERE WERE SCRIBES and scribes in Israel. A village scribe might be the man who wrote up marriage contracts, bills of sale, and petitions for hearing to the King's court or to the Jewish Sanhedrin in Jerusalem. Such a man might write letters for anyone and everyone who paid him to do so, and he could read what came in, and see that the contents were understood by those who lacked a facility for language. Amongst our people far and wide, reading was common; but writing took experience and skills. And so we had those kinds of scribes. There were three or four of them in Nazareth.

Then there was the other kind of scribe, the great Scribe who had studied the Law, who had spent years in the libraries of the Temple, the Scribe who knew the traditions of the Pharisees, the Scribe who could dispute with the Essenes when they criticized the Temple or the priesthood, a Scribe who could instruct the boys who came to the Temple to learn all that was contained in the Law and the Prophets and in the Psalms and in the writings, hundreds and hundreds of books of writing apart from these.

Hananel of Cana had been such a great Scribe. He'd spent his early years in the Temple; and he had been a judge for many years in different courts that convened to try cases from Capernaum to Sepphoris.

But he was too old now for such things, and he had long ago prepared for this day by building the largest and most beautiful house in Cana. It was large because it contained all his books, which numbered in the thousands. And it had once contained the rooms of his sons and daughters. But they'd gone to the grave long ago, leaving him alone in this world with occasional letters from a granddaughter who lived in Jerusalem and letters perhaps, no one knew, from a grandson who had stormed out of the house in a rage against its rules two years ago.

James and Little Joseph, Little Simon, Little Judas, and my cousins and nephews and I—we had built Hananel's house. And it had been one of the joys of those years, laying floors of gorgeous marble, and painting walls in rich colors of red or deep blue, and decorating them with borders of florets and twining ivy.

The house was sprawling, Greek in design, with an inner court surrounded by open rooms meant to provide the very finest setting for the company who came to see Hananel—the highborn of Galilee, the scholars from Alexandria, the Pharisees and Scribes from Babylon. And indeed the house had been filled with such people for many years, and it was a common thing to see these travelers on the road to visit Hananel, to bring him books, to sit in the gardens of the house or beneath its painted ceilings and talk to him about the goings-on of the world and about matters of the Law which men so loved to discuss when gathered together.

But as death had emptied the house, as the granddaughter in Jerusalem retired a widow and childless to live with her husband's people, the house grew quiet around the old man.

And so it stood, a monument to the way in which life

might be lived, but was not lived, a shining fortress on the hill above the small gathering of houses that made up the town of Cana.

As I stood at the iron gate, a gate my brothers and I had put on its hinges, I looked out on the land that belonged to Hananel—for as far as I could see. And beyond that, I knew, surrounding the distant peak of Nazareth, were the lands of Shemayah.

A great many who lived in the surrounding towns worked these lands—these fields, these orchards, these vineyards. But the greatest pride of the two men was their olive groves. Everywhere I saw these groves and beside them the inevitable mikvah where the men bathed before the harvest because the oil from these olives had to be pure if it was to go to the Temple in Jerusalem, if it was to be sold to the pious Jews of Galilee, or Judea, or the many cities of the Empire.

Students now and then came to Hananel, but he was rumored not to be a patient teacher.

As I came into the house, I saw he was with one of those students now, a young man named Nathanael, who sat quite literally at the old man's feet in the grand room of the house at the far end of the courtyard. I scarcely knew the young man. I'd seen him now and then on the pilgrimages.

I had a look at them both from a distance as I sat in the foyer. A patient slave washed my feet, as I took a drink of water from a limestone cup and gratefully gave it back to him.

"Yeshua," said the slave under his breath. "He's in a rage today. I don't know why he sent for you, but be careful."

"He didn't send for me, my friend," I said. "Please go in and tell him I must speak to him. And I'll wait as long as I have to."

The slave wandered off, shaking his head, and I sat for a

moment enjoying the warmth of the sun as it came through the high lattice above the door. The mosaic floor of the courtyard had been our finest work. I studied it now, and I looked slowly at the full, rich potted trees that surrounded the mirrorlike pond in the center.

No pagan nymphs or gods decorated these floors or walls, not for this devout Jew. Only the permissible designs, circles, curlicues, and lilies, which once we had so carefully laid out to decorate a perfect symmetry.

All this was open to the sky, the dusty rainless sky. It was open to the cold. But for a moment it was possible to forget the drought, to look at the shimmering sheet of water, or the fruit glistening on the trees, fresh with droplets from a slave's pitcher, and think that the world outside wasn't parched and dying. And that young men weren't still flowing, by the hundreds, into the distant city of Caesarea.

The sun had warmed the floors and the walls; the heat was sweet and I could feel it creeping over my hands and even my feet as I sat in the shadows.

Finally the young man Nathanael got up and went out, without noticing me. The gate shut with the usual chink.

I said a silent prayer and followed the slave through the small forest of well-watered figs and palms and into the grand library.

A stool had been set there for me, a simple folding stool of leather and polished wood, very fancy, and very comfortable.

I remained standing.

The old man sat at his desk, in a cross-legged Roman chair, his back to the lattice, amid silken pillows, and Babylonian rugs, scrolls heaped before him and bulging from the bookshelves all around him. The walls were bookshelves. His desk had ink and pens and bits and scraps of paper, and a wax tablet. And a stack of codices—those little parchment books with stitched bindings that the Romans called *membrane*.

The sunshine twinkled in the lattice. The palm fronds outside scratched against it.

The old man was now completely bald, and his eyes very pale, almost gray. He was very cold, though the brazier was heaped high, and the air was as warm as it was fragrant with the scent of cedar.

"Come closer," he said.

I did as he asked. I bowed.

"Yeshua bar Joseph," I said, "from Nazareth, to see you, my lord. I'm grateful that you've received me."

"What do you want!" he said. His voice had leapt out of him sharply with these words. "Well, say it!" he declared. "Tell me."

"On a matter concerning our kinsman, my lord," I said, "Shemayah bar Hyrcanus and his daughter, Avigail."

He sat back or, I should say, collapsed in his heap of wrappings. He looked away from me, then pulled the blankets up tighter around him.

"What news do you have from Caesarea!" he asked.

"None, my lord, that hasn't reached Cana. The Jews are assembled there. It's been many days now. Pilate does not come out to speak to the crowd. The crowd won't go away. That's the last I heard this morning before I left Nazareth."

"Nazareth," he whispered crossly, "where they stone children on the say-so of other children."

I bowed my head.

"Yeshua, sit down on that stool. Don't stand in front of me like a servant. You didn't come here to repair these floors, did you? You came on a matter of our families."

I moved to the stool, and slowly sat as he'd told me to do. I was looking up at him. Perhaps six feet lay between us. He was higher because of all the cushions he required, and I could see that his hand was withered and thin, that the bones of his face all but poked through the flesh.

The air here, near the brazier, was intoxicatingly warm. So was the sun falling on my face, and on the back of his head.

"My lord, I come on a distressing errand," I said.

"That fool Jason," he said, "the nephew of Jacimus, is he in Caesarea?"

"Yes, my lord," I said.

"And has he written from Caesarea?"

"Only the news I've told you, my lord. I spoke with the Rabbi this morning."

Silence. I waited. Finally, I said,

"My lord, what is it you want to know?"

"Simply this," he said. "Whether or not Jason has heard from my grandson, Reuben. Whether or not Jason speaks of my grandson, Reuben. I will not humble myself to ask that wretch such a question, but you I ask in confidence under my roof, here in my house. Does that miserable Greek wanderer speak of my grandson, Reuben?"

"No, my lord. I know they were friends. That's all I know."

"And my grandson could be married this day in Rome or in Antioch or wherever he is, married to a foreign woman, and this to spite me." He bowed his head. His demeanor changed. He seemed to have forgotten I was there, or not to care who I was, had he ever cared. "I brought this on myself," he said. "I did this to myself, put the sea between him and me, put the world between me and the woman he marries and the fruit of her womb, I did this."

I waited.

He turned and looked at me as if waking from a dream.

"And you are going to speak to me of this poor girl, this child, Avigail, whom the bandits pulled off her feet, whom the bandits so brutally frightened."

"Yes, my lord," I said.

"Why? Why come here to me with this, and why you, what do you want me to do about it?" he asked. "Do you think I'm not heartsick for the girl? Pity the man who has a daughter that beautiful, with such a ringing laugh, with such a lovely gift for song and words. I watched her grow up on the road between here and the Temple. Well, what is it, what do you want from me!"

"I'm sorry, my lord, to cause you grief—."

"Stop it, go on. Why are you here, Yeshua, the Sinless!"

"My lord, the girl is dying in her house. She takes no food and nothing to drink. And the girl is unharmed, except for the insult to her and to her father."

"The fool," he said disgustedly. "Sent for the midwife for his own daughter! Refusing the word of his own daughter!"

I waited.

"Do you know why my son left for Rome, Yeshua bar Joseph? Did that madman Jason tell you?"

"No, my lord. It's never been mentioned."

"Well, you knew that he left."

"I did, but not why," I explained.

"Because he wanted to marry," said the old man. His eyes glittered as he turned to look away. "He wanted to marry, and not into the Jerusalem family to which I had pointed my finger, but a village girl, a lovely little village girl. Avigail."

I lowered my eyes, and I sat still. Again I waited.

"You didn't know this?"

"No, my lord. No one told me," I said. "Perhaps no one knows."

"Oh, they all know," he said. "Jacimus knows."

"Hmmmm, does he?"

"Yes, indeed he does and he knew at the time, and my grandson, on his own, without my blessing, went calling on

Shemayah, and that girl no more than thirteen at the time," he said excitedly. He turned this way and that, eyes roving. "And I, I said no, you will not, you will not marry such a young child, not now, and not from Nazareth, I don't care that her father is rich, that her mother was rich, that she's rich. I don't care, you will marry the girl of my choosing of your kindred in Jerusalem. And now this happens! And you come to me about it."

Again his eyes settled on me and he seemed to see me for the first time. I merely looked at him.

"Still playing the village fool, I see," he said. He peered at me as if trying to memorize my face and features.

"My lord, will you write a letter for Avigail, a letter to our kindred in Jerusalem or Sepphoris, or wherever they might be best suited to receive her, to offer her a home of which she can be part? The girl's blameless. The girl's clever. The girl's sweet, and gentle. The girl's modest."

He was surprised. Then he laughed.

"What makes you think Shemayah will let her out of his grip?"

"My lord, if you find such a place, and you write a letter stating this case, if you yourself, Hananel the Judge, should come with us, with the Rabbi and with my father Joseph, we can surely see to it that Avigail is safely taken away to some place very far from Nazareth. A man can say no to the Rabbi in Nazareth. He can say no to the elders in Nazareth. It's not easy to say no to Hananel of Cana, regardless of what's happened before—and I don't know that Shemayah knows anything about your grandson and what happened between you."

"He was for the match," came the flashing response. "Shemayah was for it until my grandson admitted he didn't have my blessing or permission."

"My lord, someone must do something to save this child. She's dying."

I stood up.

"Tell me to whom I can go, what kindred in Sepphoris," I said. "Give a note of introduction. Tell me what household. I'll go there."

"Don't get yourself into a perfect rage," he said, sneering. "Sit down. And be quiet. I'll find a place for her. I know the place. I know more than one."

I sighed, and I murmured a small prayer of thanks.

"Tell me, O pious one," he said. "Why haven't you, yourself, asked for the girl? And don't tell me she's too good for a carpenter. Right now, she's good for nothing."

"She is good," I said. "She's blameless."

"And you, the child of Mary of Joachim and Anna, tell me. I've always wanted to know. Are you a man beneath those robes? A man? You understand me?"

I stared at him. I could feel the heat in my face. I could feel myself begin to tremble, but not to the extent that he could see it. I refused to look away from him.

"A man like other men?" he asked. "You do understand why I ask. Oh, it's not that you don't marry. The prophet Jeremiah didn't marry. But if memory serves me right, and it always does, and I do remember talking in this very place, though not in this house, in another house, with your grandfather Joachim at the time—and if memory serves me right from those days and it does—the angel who announced your birth to your shivering little mother wasn't simply some angel fallen from the Heavenly Court, it was none other than the angel Gabriel."

Silence.

We stared at one another.

"Gabriel," he said to me. He raised his chin slightly and

arched his eyebrows. "The angel Gabriel himself. He came to speak to your mother and to none other, except, as we all know—the prophet Daniel."

The warmth beat in my face; it beat in my chest. I could feel it in the palms of my hands.

"You press me like a grape, my lord," I said, "between your thumb and forefinger." *And I know that when pressed in this manner, I may say strange things, things I don't even think in the course of my day-to-day work, things I don't even think when I'm alone . . . or dreaming.*

"So I do," he said. "Because I despise you."

"So it seems, my lord."

"Why don't you jump to your feet again?"

"I stay because I'm on an errand."

He laughed with immense satisfaction. He curled his fingers under his chin and looked around him, but not at the heaps of books, or the lattices with their flashes of light and green, or at the pools of light on the marble floor, or the thin sweet smoke rising from the bronze brazier.

What does it take to ransom Avigail?

"Well, you certainly do love this child, don't you?" he asked. "Either that or you are a fool, as people say, but only some people, I should add."

"What must we do to help her?"

"Don't you want to know why I despise you?" he asked.

"Is it your wish that I should know?"

"I know all the stories about you."

"So it seems."

"About the strange doings when you were born, how your family fled to Egypt, about the miserable massacre of those babies in Bethlehem by that madman who called himself our King, about the things you can do."

"Things I can do? I laid this marble floor," I said. "I'm a carpenter. That's the sort of thing I can do."

"Precisely," he said. "And that's why I despise you. And anyone else would too if they had the memory that I have!" He lifted his finger as though instructing a child. "Samson's birth was foretold, not by the angel Gabriel, but by an angel for certain. And Samson was a man. And we know his mighty deeds and repeat them generation after generation. Where are your mighty deeds? Where are your defeated enemies lying dead in heaps, or where are the ruins of the heathen temples that you've brought down with the strength of your arm?"

The heat in me burnt blindingly fierce. I had risen to my feet, and knocked the stool aside without meaning to do it. I stood there before him but I didn't see him and I didn't see the room.

It was as if I was remembering something, something forgotten all my life. But this wasn't a memory. No, it was something altogether different.

Heathen temples, where are your heathen temples. In no set place or time, I saw temples, and I saw them falling, I heard them falling, collapsing, as air and form and light shifted, as clouds of dust rose like the boiling sky of a tempest, a sky that went on forever—and this shifting, this breaking, this fierce and deafening ruin, moved on like the ever-changing and ceaseless sea.

I closed my eyes. Memories threatened the purity of this inner vision. Memories of my boyhood in Alexandria, of the Roman processions weaving their way towards their shrines with clouds of rose petals swirling in the air and the steady beat of drums, the shiver of sistrums. I heard the singing of the women, and I saw a golden god drifting forward beneath a wavering canopy—and then the vision returned, sweeping up the memory in its mighty current, the vision so huge and vague that it was shaking the whole world as if the mountains around all the great sea were rumbling and spewing fire, and the altars were falling. The altars were crashing down into pieces.

All of this dissolved. The room came back.

I turned and looked at the old man. He looked like leather and bone. No meanness in him. He seemed frail and like a lily held too close to the brazier, like something withering, burning up.

A deep piercing sense of his misery came to me, his years alone in grief for those he'd lost, his fear of failing eyes and failing fingers and failing reason and failing hope.

Unbearable.

A humming came to my ears, a humming from every room of the house, a humming from beyond the house, from all the rooms of all the houses—the frail, the sick, the weary, the suffering, the bitter.

Unbearable. But I can bear it. I will bear it.

I'd been looking at him for a long while, but only now realized he was stricken with sadness. He was silently imploring me.

"Come here to me," he begged.

I stood a step nearer, then another step. I watched him reach for my hand and lift my hand. How silken his hand felt, the skin of his palm so thin. He looked up at me.

"When you were twelve years old," he said, "when you came to the Temple to be presented to Israel, I was there. I was one of the Scribes who examined you and all the boys with you. Do you remember me from that time?"

I didn't answer.

"We were questioning you, all you boys, about the Book of Samuel, do you remember this, in particular?" he asked.

He was eager and careful with his words. His hand clung to mine. "We were speaking of the story of King Saul, after he's been anointed for the kingship by the prophet Samuel . . . but before anyone knew that Saul was to be King." He stopped, and ran his tongue over his dry lips. But his eyes were fastened to mine.

"Saul fell in with a group of prophets on the road, you remember, and the Spirit came over Saul and Saul went into ecstasy and Saul fell down into a trance among the prophets. And those looking on, those who saw this sight, one of them asked, 'And who is their father?' "

I didn't say anything.

"We asked you boys, we asked you all, to think of that story and tell us, What did this man mean who asked of Saul, 'And who is their father?' The other boys were quick to say that prophets had to come from families of prophets, and that Saul did not, and so it was natural for someone to ask this question."

I kept silent.

"Your answer," he said, "was different from that of the other boys. Do you remember? You said it was an insult, this question. It was an insult from those who had never known ecstasy or the power of the Spirit, those who envied the ones who did. The man who mocked was saying, 'Who are you, Saul, and what is your right to be among the prophets?' "

He studied me, holding my hand as tight as before.

"You remember?"

"I do," I said.

"You said, 'Men scorn what they can't grasp. They suffer in their longing for it.' "

Silence from me.

He drew his left hand out of his robes and now he held my hand with both his hands.

"Why didn't you stay with us in the Temple?" he asked. "We begged you to do it." He sighed. "Think of what you might have done if you had remained in the Temple and studied; think of the boy you were! If only you'd devoted your life to what is written, think what you might have done. I took such delight in you, and we all did, and Old Berekhiah and Sherebiah from Nazareth, how they loved you and wanted you to stay. But what have you become! A carpenter—one of a gang of carpenters. Men who make floors, walls, benches, and tables."

Very slowly I tried to free my hand, but he wouldn't let me go. I moved slowly to his left and saw even more of the light spill down on his upturned face.

"The world swallowed you," he said bitterly. "You left the Temple and the world simply swallowed you. That's what the world does. It swallows everything. One woman's angel is another man's scornful tale. Grass grows over the ruins of villages until one can find nothing of them and trees sprout from the very stones where great houses, houses like this one, once stood. All these books are falling to pieces, aren't they? Look, see the bits of parchment all over my robes. The world swallows the Word of God. You should have stayed and studied Torah! What would your grandfather Joachim say if he knew what you've become?"

He sat back. He let me go. His lips curved into a sneer. He looked up at me though his gray brows were drawn down into a frown. He motioned for me to go away from him.

I stood there.

"Why does the world swallow the Word of God?" I asked. He couldn't hear the heat in my voice. "Why?" I asked. "Are we not a holy people, are we not to be a bright and shining light to the nations? Are we not to bring salvation to the whole world?"

"That is what we are!" he said. "Our Temple is the greatest Temple in the Empire. Who doesn't know this?"

"Our Temple is one of a thousand temples, my lord," I said.

Again came that flash, seemingly of memory, buried memory of some great agitated moment, but it was no memory. "A thousand temples throughout the world," I said, "and every day sacrifice is offered to a thousand gods from one end of the Empire to the other."

He glared at me.

I went on,

"All around us this happens, in the land of Israel this happens. It happens in Tyre, in Sidon, in Ashkelon; it happens in Caesarea Philippi; it happens in Tiberias. And in Antioch and in Corinth and in Rome and in the woods of the great north and in the wilds of Britannia." I took a slow breath. "Are we the light of the nations, my lord?" I demanded.

"What is all that to us!" he countered.

"What is all that? Egypt, Italy, Greece, Germania, Asia, what is all that? It's the world, my lord. That's what it is to us, it's the world to whom we are to be the light, we, our people!"

He was outraged. "What are you saying?"

"It's where I live, my lord," I said. "Not in the Temple, but in the world. And in the world, I learn what the world is and what the world will teach, and I am of the world. The world's made of wood and stone and iron, and I work in it. No, not in the Temple. In the world. And I study Torah; and I pray with the assembly; and on the feasts I go to Jerusalem to stand before the Lord—in the Temple—but this is in the world, all this. In the world. And when it is time for me to do what the Lord has sent me to do in this world, this world which belongs to Him, this world of wood and stone and iron and grass and air, He will reveal it to me. And what this carpenter shall yet build in this world on that day, the Lord knows, and the Lord shall reveal it."

He was speechless.

I took a step back from him. I turned and stared ahead of me. I saw the dust moving in the rays of the noon sunshine. Sparkling in lattices above bookshelves and bookshelves. I thought I saw images in the dust, things moving with purpose, things airy and immense yet guided and patient in their movement.

It seemed the room was filled with others, the beating of their hearts, but they were invisible hearts or not even hearts. Not hearts like my heart or his heart, of flesh and blood.

Leaves rattled at the windows and a cold draft crept across the shining floor. I felt removed and at the same time there, under his roof, standing before him, with my back to him, and I was drifting, yet anchored, and content to be so.

The anger washed out of me.

I turned and looked at him.

He was calm and wondering. He sat collected amid his robes. He sat peering at me as if from a great and safe distance.

When he spoke, it was a murmur.

"All these years," he said, "as I've watched you on the road to Jerusalem, I've wondered, 'What does he think? What does he know?' "

"Do you have an answer?"

"I have hope," he whispered.

I thought about this, and then slowly I nodded.

"I'll write the letter this afternoon," he said. "I have a student here to take the dictation for me. The letter will reach my cousins in Sepphoris this evening. They are widows. They're kind. They'll welcome her."

I bowed and placed my fingers together to show my thanks and my respect. I started to go.

"Come back in three days," he said. "I'll have an answer from them or from someone else. I'll have it in hand. And I'll go with you to see Shemayah on this matter. And if you see the girl herself, you will tell her that all her family—we are all asking after her."

"Thank you, my lord," I said.

I walked fast on the road to Sepphoris.

I wanted to be with my brothers, I wanted to be at work. I wanted to be laying stones one after another, and pouring the grout and smoothing the boards and hammering the nails. I wanted anything but to be with a man with a clever tongue.

But what had he said that my own brothers hadn't said in their own way, or that Jason hadn't said? Oh, he'd been full of privilege and riches and the arrogant power that he held to help Avigail.

But they were asking me the same questions. They were all saying the same things.

I didn't want to go over it in my mind. I didn't want to go over the things he'd said or what I'd seen or felt. And most especially I didn't want to ponder what I'd said to him.

But as I reached the city with all its engulfing voices, its wondrous pounding and clattering and chatter, a thought came to me.

The thought was fresh and like the conversation I'd had.

I'd been looking all this while for signs that rain would come, hadn't I? I'd been looking at the sky, and at the distant trees, and feeling the wind, and the chill of the wind, and hoping to catch just a kiss of moisture on my face.

But maybe I was seeing signs of something else altogether different. Something was indeed coming. It had to be. Here, all around me, were the signals of its approach. It was a build-

ing, a pressure, a series of signals of something inevitable—
something like the rain for which we'd all prayed, yet something vastly beyond the rain—and something that would
take the decades of my life, yes, the years reckoned in feasts
and new moons, and even the hours and the minutes—even
every single second I'd ever lived—and make use of it.

12

THE FOLLOWING MORNING, Old Bruria and Aunt Esther tried to get word to Avigail, but could get no answer.

By the time we came back from the city that evening, Silent Hannah had come in. She sat now broken and small and shivering beside Joseph who kept his hand on her bowed head. She looked like a tiny woman under her woolen veils.

"What's the matter with her?" James asked.

My mother said, "She says Avigail is dying."

"Give me some water to wash my hands," I said. "I need the ink and parchment."

I sat down and put a board over my knees for a desk. And I grasped the pen, amazed at how difficult it was. It had been a long time since I'd written anything, and the calluses on my fingers were thick and my hand felt rough and even unsteady. Unsteady.

Ah, what a discovery that was.

I dipped the pen and scratched out the words, simply and fast, and in the smallest possible letters. "You eat and drink now because I say you must. You get up and you take all the water that you can now because I say you must. You eat what you can. I do all that I can do on your behalf, and you do this now for me and for those who love you. Letters have been sent from those who love you to those who love you. You will soon be away from here. Say nothing to your father. Do as I tell you."

I went to Silent Hannah and gave her the parchment. I gestured as I spoke. "From me to Avigail. From me. You give it to her."

She shook her head. She was terrified.

I made the ominous gesture for a scowling Shemayah. I gestured to my eyes. I said: "He can't read it. See? Look at how small are the letters! You give it to Avigail!"

She got up and ran out quickly.

Hours passed. Silent Hannah didn't come back.

But shouts from the street roused all of us from our semi-sleep. We rushed out to discover that the signal fires had just reported the news: peace in Caesarea.

And Pontius Pilate had sent word to Jerusalem to remove the offensive ensigns from the Holy City.

Soon the street was lighted up as it had been on the night the men rode out. People were drinking, dancing, and locking arms. But no one knew the particulars as yet, and no one expected to know. The fires gave the word that the men were returning to their homes all over the country.

There was no sign of life in the house of Shemayah, not even the glimmer of a lamp beneath the door or in the chink of a window.

My aunts used this festive occasion to hammer on the door.

It did no good.

"I pray Silent Hannah's asleep next to her," said my mother.

The Rabbi called us all to the synagogue to give thanks for the peace.

But no one really rested easy until the next afternoon, by which time Jason and several of the men, hiring mounts for the whole way, had reached Nazareth.

We threw down our bundles, fed the animals, and made for the synagogue to pray and to hear the story of what had happened.

As before, the crowd was much too big for the building. People were lighting torches and lanterns in the street. The sky was quickly darkening.

I caught a glimpse of Jason, who was bursting with excitement and gesturing wildly to his uncle. But all begged him to stop and wait and tell the tale to the whole village.

Finally benches were dragged out of the synagogue and up the slope, and soon some fifteen hundred or so men and women were massed in the open area, torch begetting torch, as Jason made his way up to the place of honor, along with his companions.

I couldn't see Silent Hannah anywhere. Of course Shemayah was not there, and certainly there was no sign of Avigail. But then, again, it was difficult to tell.

People were embracing and clapping their hands, kissing one another, dancing. The children were in a paroxysm of delight. And James was crying. My brothers had brought Joseph and Alphaeus along slowly. Some of the other elders were also late in coming.

Jason waited. He stood on the bench, embracing his companion, and only then as the torches drew in, clearly illuminating them both, did I realize that the companion was Hananel's grandson, Reuben.

My mother recognized him at the same moment, and the word spread in a whisper through all of us, as we stood crowded together.

I hadn't told them any of what Hananel had said to me. I

had not even asked the Rabbi why he hadn't warned me that Hananel's grandson had once come to court Avigail.

But all knew how the grandfather had grieved for two years for this lost son who had gone abroad, and soon the name "Reuben bar Daniel bar Hananel" was being whispered everywhere.

He was elegant, this one, and beautifully dressed in linen robes just as was Jason, with the same barbered beard and anointed hair, though both were thoroughly soiled from the long hard ride, and neither seemed to care about this.

Finally the whole town shouted for the men to tell the story.

"Six days," declared Jason, holding up his fingers so that we might count. "Six days we stood before the palace of the Governor and demanded that he remove his brazen and blasphemous images from our Holy City."

Shouts of wonder and approval rose in a soft roar.

" 'Oh, but this would give injury to our great Tiberius,' the man told us," Jason cried. "And we to him, 'He's always respected our laws in the past.' And understand that for every day we remained firm, more and more men and women came to join us. Understand that Caesarea was overflowing! In and out of the palace of the Governor went the men who presented our petitions, and no sooner were they dismissed than they returned and presented them again, until at last the man had had his fill of it.

"And all the while soldiers had come pouring in, soldiers taking up their stands at every gate, at every door, and all along the walls that bounded the pavement before the judgment seat."

The crowd gave a loud roar before he could go on, but he gestured for quiet, and continued.

"At last, sitting there before the great mass of us he

declared that the images would not be removed. And giving the signal brought his soldiers to full arms against us! Swords were drawn. Daggers lifted. We saw ourselves on every side surrounded by his men, and we saw our deaths right in front of us—."

He stopped. And as the crowd murmured and shouted and finally roared, he gestured for quiet again and came to the finish.

"Did we not remember the advice our elders had given us?" Jason asked. "Did we need to be told that we are a people of peace? Did we need to be cautioned that Roman soldiers would soon hold our breath in their hands, no matter how many of us had banded together?"

The shouts came from all around.

"On the ground, we threw ourselves," Jason cried. "On the very ground, and we bowed our heads, and we bared our necks to those swords—all of us. Hundreds of us did this, I tell you. Thousands of us. We bared our necks, all of us, to a man, fearlessly and silently, and those who were left to speak told the Governor what he already knew, that we should surely die—all of us, to a man, as we knelt there!— before we would see our laws overturned, our customs abolished."

Jason folded his arms and looked from right to left as the cries rang out and slowly rolled into one great song of jubilation. Nodding and smiling, he waved to the little boys who clamored at the foot of the bench. And Reuben stood beside him, as filled with pure happiness as he was.

My uncle Cleopas was crying; so was James. So were all the men.

"And what did the great Roman Governor do in the face of this spectacle?" cried Jason. "At the undeniable sight of so many ready to give their lives for the protection of our most sacred laws, the man rose to his feet and ordered his soldiers to put away the weapons they held at our throats, the blades flashing in the sun everywhere before him. 'They shall not die!' he declared. 'Not for piety! I will not shed their blood, not one drop! Give the signal. The soldiers are to remove our ensigns from within the walls of their sacred city!' "

Cries of thanksgiving filled the air. Prayers and acclamation. People went down on their knees in the grass. The noise was so great that nothing further could have possibly been heard from Jason or Reuben or anyone for that matter.

Fists were in the air, people were dancing again, and the women were sobbing now, as if only now could they sink down onto the grass and let their full fear flow from their hearts and into the arms of one another.

The Rabbi who stood near the summit beside Jason bowed his head and began the prayers, but we couldn't hear him. People began to sing psalms of thanksgiving. Bits of melody and prayer floated and mingled all around us.

Little Mary sobbed against the breast of my uncle Cleopas, her father-in-law, and James held his wife, kissing her forehead silently as the tears came down his face. I hugged Little Isaac to me and Yaqim and all of Avigail's children, who were with us now, even as I knew it meant that Silent Hannah and Avigail had not come to this crowd, no, not even for this.

We were all kissing one another. Wineskins were passed. People had broken into long discourses on how this had seemed or that had been, and Jason and Reuben struggled through the press, besieged for the greater details, though both men now appeared completely spent and ready to collapse if given the opportunity.

Joseph clasped my hand and James' hand. Our brothers and their wives made a circle, and the little children stood in our midst. My mother had her arms around my shoulders and her head against my back.

" 'Sacrifice and offerings You do not desire, O Lord,' " said Joseph, " 'but ears open to obedience You've given us. Burnt offerings You did not demand. So I said, "Here I am; Your commands for me are written in the scroll. To do Your will is my life; my Lord, Your law is in my heart. I announced Your deeds to a great assembly. . . ." ' "

It took us a long time to make our way home.

The street was choked with revelers, and it was plain as well that other men were arriving, others who'd hired mounts for the hard ride, and we could hear the sharp unmistakable cries of those who were being reunited.

Suddenly Jason, bright faced and smelling of wine, caught up with us, his hand over James' shoulder.

"Your boys are well, they're well indeed and stood straight and strong with us, both of them, Menachim and Shabi, and I tell you all of the men of your house stood firm. Silas, and Levi, of course, I expected it, who didn't, but little Shabi I tell you, and Young Cleopas, and every man—." And on he went, kissing James and then my uncles, and kissing the hands that Joseph lifted in blessing.

We'd reached the gate to the courtyard when Reuben of Cana caught up with us, and he tried to take his leave of Jason now, but Jason protested. They passed the wineskin between them and offered it to us. I waved it away.

"Why are you not happy!" Jason demanded of me.

"We are happy, all of us are happy," I said. "Reuben, it's been many years. Come inside, refresh yourself."

"No, he's coming home with me," said Jason. "My uncle wouldn't hear of it if he didn't lodge with us. Reuben, what's the matter with you, you can't ride out for Cana now."

"But I must do that, Jason, and you know I must,"

Reuben said. He looked to us as he took his leave, nodding to us. "My grandfather hasn't seen me in two years," he said. Joseph answered Reuben's nod with his own. All the older men nodded.

Jason shrugged. "Don't come to me tomorrow," said Jason, "and tell me the sad story of how you woke up and found yourself—in the great city of Cana!"

All the young men around them broke into laughter.

Reuben seemed to melt away in the shadows, amid the happy voices, and the crush of those who wanted to clap Jason and clasp his hand, and all those struggling to come and go.

Finally, having taken our leave fifty times over, we did go into the house.

Old Bruria had gone before us and lighted the coals, and the aroma of the hot pottage was strong and inviting.

As I helped Joseph to take his place against the wall, I saw Silent Hannah.

Amid all the comings and goings, she stood stock-still, staring only at me, as if no one else brushed past her.

She looked weary and old, positively old—like an ancient one, so thin and so stooped and making fists of her hands that held on to her veil as if it were a rope in the sea. She shook her head No. It was a slow, despairing negation.

"Did you give her the writing?" I asked. "Did she read it?"

Her face was blank. She made a gesture with her right hand, over and over, almost as if she were scratching at the air.

My mother said, "She gave the letter to Avigail. She doesn't know if Avigail read it."

"Go now to his house," said Old Bruria. "You, Cleopas, go! Go and take your daughter-in-law with you. Go now and bang on his door. Tell him you've come to give him this news."

"Everyone who has passed has knocked," said James. "Jason was pounding on his door just now, as we came in. It's enough for tonight. Maybe the old fool will wander out on his own. The noise will keep him awake all night, one way or the other."

"We could somehow knock in his door, you know," said Cleopas. "All of us, dancing and drinking, we could, just sort of knock in his door, and then what, of course, we'd tell him we were so sorry, but with this . . ."

He broke off. No one had the heart for such a thing.

"This is no night to tell Jason," said James. "But we can count on him tomorrow to knock in that door if we must."

We all agreed to that. And we knew that his uncle, the Rabbi, would undoubtedly tell him everything.

13

THERE WAS TO BE NO WORK the next day. It was a festival, a celebration, and a thanksgiving unto the Lord for the Governor's decision, and those who were wont to drink did so, but mainly people went from house to house, to talk over the grand event, which was to some the triumph of the people, and to the others the humiliation of the Governor, and to the older men simply the will of God.

James, because he could not keep still, swept the stables and the courtyard twice, and I, because I could not keep still if James did not keep still, watered and fed the donkeys, went out to see how bad things were with the vegetable garden, came back thinking it best to say nothing about the tender crops dying there, looked at the cold sky, and decided to go to Cana.

Of course this was no day to prevail on Hananel to do anything on behalf of anyone. His beloved grandson was home, and surely he should be left to savor this and give thanks as he chose to do.

But I couldn't wait. No matter what I did, no matter where I went, I saw Avigail in my mind's eye, Avigail, alone in her dark room. I saw Avigail lying on the floor, and sometimes I saw Avigail's dull eyes.

The little town of Cana, much smaller than Nazareth, seemed just as noisy with festivities, and I passed along unnoticed as everywhere men gathered to drink and talk, and people even took their noon meal on the dried grass under the trees. The wind was not so bad for this. And it seemed people had forgotten about the drought altogether; they had won a great victory over something they feared even more.

Hananel's house was full of commotion. Preparations for a feast were taking place. Men were busy bringing in baskets of fruit. I could smell the roasting lamb.

I went to the door, and found the old slave who'd greeted me when I'd last come.

"Listen, I can't disturb the master on this day," I said. "But you must get a message to him for me, please."

"Of course I will, Yeshua, but you must come in. The master's brimming with happiness. Reuben has come home, safe and sound, this very morning."

"Tell the master only that I came, and that I wish him joy at this time," I said. "And tell him I wait for word on the matter as before. Will you do this for me? Whisper to him, that's all I ask. Put it in his mind when you can."

I went off before the slave could protest, and hadn't gotten halfway home to Nazareth when Jason met me on the road. He was on a horse, an unusual sight, and perhaps it was the mount he'd hired for the ride from Caesarea. At once he jumped down and came to me.

Without any preliminaries he launched into a tirade.

"The man's a fool to do this to his own daughter, to lock her up and starve her, to wish that for this, this, she should die."

"I know," I said. And then I told him as quickly as I could that Hananel of Cana had written to Avigail's family elsewhere. "And so we wait now for word."

"Where are you going?" he demanded.

"Home," I said. "I can't pester the man on the day of his grandson's homecoming. I left a message. That was all I could do."

"Well, I'm on my way there now to dine with them," said Jason. "The old man himself sent for me. I'll see to it that he remembers this. I'll see to it he remembers nothing else."

"Jason, be wise," I said. "He's sent the letters on her behalf. Don't come like a tempest into the house with this. Be happy that he's invited you to celebrate under his roof."

Jason nodded.

"Before you go I want you to tell me all of it," he said, "what those bandits did. They flung her to the ground on her face, that's what my uncle said—."

"What does it matter now?" I asked. "I cannot do this. I won't relive it. You go on. Find me tomorrow and I'll tell you if you must know."

By late afternoon, Menachim and Shabi had come home, and almost all of the young men who'd gone away. The house was full of arguments and recriminations. Uncle Cleopas was furious with his sons Joseph and Judas and Simon. They stood quietly by, enduring the lecture, but confident with their secretive glances and smiles that they had been a party to a splendid thing.

James would have whipped Shabi, but his wife, Mara, stopped him.

I slipped away.

Outside Shemayah's house, Little Isaac and Yaqim stood watch grimly at a door that wouldn't open. Silent Hannah came up from the market with a small basket, heaped with fruit and bread. She looked at me as if she didn't know me. She gave a knock that was obviously a signal, and the door opened and I saw the dour face of the old serving woman before the door was slammed closed again.

I went on up the street and down and towards the stream. There was now so little water running down from the basins that the bed of the stream was gray, like everything else, with dust. The sun found sudden bursts of light here and there where the water still ran, deep and secretive and slow.

I went to the basin and slowly washed my hands and my face.

Then I went to the grove.

I knelt for a while and I prayed to the Lord for Avigail. I knew I'd weep, and only slowly did it occur to me that weeping here was perfectly acceptable. There was no one to see it but the Lord. And I gave way finally. "Father in Heaven, how has this happened? How is it that this girl is suffering when she's innocent, and how could my blunder have only made it worse?"

At last exhaustion came over me, almost a sweet exhaustion because it pushed all anxiety ahead of it, and I collapsed on the soft bed of moldering leaf.

I crooked my arm for a pillow and I went effortlessly into sleep.

It wasn't deep sleep. It was a kind of lovely melting into the soft sounds around me, the crunch of the freshly fallen leaves beneath me, and the whisper of those overhead. Soon I could no longer hear my own heart. The sweetest fragrances came to me. Half in sleep I wondered at it, that in this awful drought, little things, fragrant things, still blossomed in sun and in shadow, and these things were near to me.

Did an hour pass? Or was it longer?

I had some sense, the sense of the man who had to rouse himself well before dark and be home again. But I didn't really know.

I shifted and turned. A small collection of sounds had

awakened me, something not usual for this place, or was it an aroma? A thick and delicious perfume.

An expensive perfume.

I didn't open my eyes yet; I did not want to shake off the web of sleep completely because I feared if I did, it wouldn't come back. And how lovely it was simply to float here, trying to define this pungent aroma, and then thinking, somewhere deep in my mind, of where I'd always caught that inviting fragrance . . . at weddings, when the jars of nard were opened for the bride and groom.

I opened my eyes. I heard the sound of garments rustling. I felt something heavy and soft drop down on my naked feet.

I turned and sat up quickly, but I was groggy. A dark mantle lay on my feet and over it a heavy black veil. Fine wool. Expensive wool. I tried to shake off the grogginess. Who was here with me and why?

I looked up, forcing the sleep off my eyes, and I saw a woman standing in front of me, a woman against the backdrop of glittering sunlight in the canopy of the trees.

Her hair was luxuriantly free. Gold on the edge of her tunic shimmered, both at her throat and along her hem. Gold embroidering, rich and thick, and from her hair and her garments came this irresistible perfume.

Avigail. Avigail in a wedding tunic. Avigail, with her hair undone and flowing down, resplendent in the light. Slowly the light defined the long smooth curve of her neck, and the naked flesh of her shoulders beneath the embroidered gold. Her tunic was unclasped. Her hands, glittering with rings and bracelets, hung at her sides.

All of her beauty blazed in the dimness as if she were a treasure discovered in secret, meant to be revealed only in secret.

And there came the awareness to me, as the last vestiges of sleep left me: she is here with me and we are alone.

All my long life I'd lived in crowded rooms, and worked in crowded rooms and crowded places, and come and gone amid crowds, and amid women who were sister, aunt, mother, cousin—daughters or wives of others, covered women, shrouded women, women wrapped to the neck with their heads covered, women swaddled in blankets or glimpsed at village weddings now and then in layers of finery, beyond cascading veils.

We were alone. The man in me knew that we were alone, and the man in me knew that I could have this woman. And all the many dreams, the tortured dreams and tortured nights of denial, might lead now into the undreamt softness of her arms.

Quickly, I climbed to my feet. I reached down for the mantle and woolen veil she'd dropped, and I picked them up.

"What are you doing?" I demanded. "What mad thought has come into your mind!" I put the mantle over her shoulders and I put the dark veil over her head. I clasped her shoulders. "You're beside yourself. You won't do this. Now, come and I'll take you home."

"No," she said. She pushed me away. "I go to the streets of the city of Tyre," she said. "I go to fling myself into those streets. No. Don't try to stop me. If you do not want for yourself here what many men will soon have for the asking, then I go now."

She turned, but I caught her wrist.

"Avigail, these are the ravings of a child," I whispered to her.

Her eyes were bitter and cold as she looked at me, but even hard as they were they began to quiver. "Yeshua, let me go," she said.

"You don't know what you're saying," I said. "The streets of Tyre! You've never even seen a city like Tyre. This is childish foolishness. You think the streets are a bosom on which you can lay your head? Avigail, you come home with me, come to my house, with my mother and my sisters. Avigail, do you think we've watched all these doings in silence, without doing anything?"

"I know what you've done," she said. "It's no use. I'm condemned and I will not starve to death under the roof of the man who's condemned me. I will not!"

"You're going to leave Nazareth," I said.

"That I will do," she declared.

"No, you don't understand. Your kinsman, Hananel of Cana, he's written letters, he . . ."

"He's come to the very door this day," she said in a dark voice. "Yes, Hananel and his grandson, Reuben, and they stood before my father and asked for my hand."

She pulled back from me. She was shaking violently.

"And do you know what my father said to those men, to Hananel of Cana and his grandson, Reuben! He refused them! 'Do you think this broken cup,' he said, 'do you think this broken cup is your pot of gold!' "

She trembled as she drew in her breath.

I was speechless.

" 'I do not put that broken cup on the auction block,' he said. My father said . . . 'I do not put my shame in the marketplace for you to buy!' "

"The man's out of his mind."

"Oh, out of his mind, yes, out of his mind that his daughter Avigail has been handled, that she's been shamed! And he would have her die in her shame! To Reuben of Cana, he said this! 'I have no daughter for you. You go.' "

She stopped. She couldn't continue. She was so badly

shaken that she couldn't get out her words. I held her shoulders.

"You are free of your father, then."

"Yes, I am," she declared.

"Then, you come home with me. You live under my roof until we get you away from this place and to our kindred in Bethany."

"Oh, what, the house of Caiaphas will take the humiliated and shamed country girl, the girl denied by her own father, her father who drove off every man who came to ask for her for two years, and has now slammed the door on Jason again, and on Reuben of Cana, Reuben who put his pride away and begged on his very knees!"

She pulled away from me.

"Avigail, I won't let you go."

She broke into sobs. I held her.

"Yeshua bar Joseph, do it," she whispered to me. "I'm here with you. Take me. I beg you. I have no shame. Take me please, Yeshua, I'm yours."

I began to weep. I couldn't stop it and it was as bad as it had been before she ever came, and as bad perhaps as her own weeping.

"Avigail, you listen to me. I tell you with God nothing is impossible, and you will be safe with my mother and my aunts. I'll send you to my sister Salome in Capernaum. My aunts will take you there. Avigail, you must come with me home."

She collapsed against me, and her sobs grew softer and softer as I held her.

"Tell me," she said finally in the smallest voice. "Yeshua, if you were to marry, would I be your bride?"

"Yes, my beautiful girl," I said. "My sweet beautiful girl."

She looked up at me, biting her lip as it quivered. "Then

take me as your harlot. Please. I don't care." She shut her eyes as they flowed with tears. "I don't care, I don't care."

"Hush, don't say another word," I said gently. I took the edge of my mantle and wiped her face. I lifted her off my chest and I made her stand on her feet. I wrapped her veil around her, and threw the end of it over her shoulder. I closed her mantle so that no one would see the gold-trimmed tunic underneath. "I'm taking you home as my sister, my dearest," I said. "You'll come with me as I said, and these words and these moments will remain locked in our hearts."

She was too weary suddenly to answer me.

"Avigail?" I said. "You look at me. You will do as I say."

She nodded.

"Look into my eyes," I said. "And you tell me who you really are. You are Avigail, the daughter of Shemayah, and you've been slandered, wickedly slandered. And we will make it right."

She nodded. The tears were gone, but the anger had left her empty and seemingly lost. It seemed for a moment, she'd fall.

I held her.

"Avigail, I will demand the elders come together. I will demand of the Rabbi that there be a village court."

She looked at me, puzzled, and then away as if these words confused her.

"This man, Shemayah, is not the judge over life and death, not even of his only daughter."

"The court?" she whispered. "The elders?"

"Yes," I said. "We will bring it out in the open. We will demand a verdict on your innocence, and with that you'll go to Capernaum or Bethany or wherever it is that's best for you."

She gazed up at me, steadily for the first time.

"This is possible?" she asked.

"Yes," I said. "It is possible. Your father has said he has no daughter. Well, then he has no authority over that daughter, and we, your kinsmen, now have that authority, and the elders have that authority. You hear what I say?"

She nodded.

"Forget the words you spoke here; they were for me, for your brother who knows the innocent and suffering child who you are."

I laid my hand on my heart.

"Lord, give to my sister a new heart," I whispered. "Lord, give her a new heart."

I remained quiet, my eyes closed, praying, holding her shoulder with my left hand.

When I opened my eyes, her face was calm. She was Avigail again, our Avigail before it had all begun.

"Come then, let's get to it," I said.

"No, you needn't go to the elders, you needn't do this. It will only humiliate my father. I'll go to Capernaum, to Salome," she said. "I'll go to Bethany, to wherever you say."

I straightened her veil again. I tried to brush some of the leaves from her veil and mantle but it was impossible. She was covered in broken bits of leaf.

"Forgive me, Yeshua," she whispered.

"For what? For being frightened? For being alone? For being hurt, and for being condemned?"

"I love you, my brother," she said.

I wanted to kiss her. I wanted just to hold her close to me again in purest love and kiss her forehead. But I didn't do it.

"You're really the child of angels," she said sadly.

"No, my beloved. I'm a man. Believe me, I am."

She smiled, the saddest most knowing smile.

"Now, you go on down to Nazareth before me, and you

walk right into my house and ask for my mother, and if you see your father, you turn and you run from him, and round about until you come again to our door."

She nodded. And she turned to go.

I stood waiting, catching my breath, drying my own tears quickly, and trying to stop my own trembling.

Then, from beyond the grove, I heard her give a sudden anguished cry.

14

I RUSHED THROUGH THE BRACKEN.

She stood only a few feet in front of me, and beyond on the descending slope there stood a loose and silent crowd.

James, Joses, Simon, my uncle Cleopas, and dozens of other men stood staring up at us. Shabi and Yaqim started forward, but the older boys took hold of them. Only Silent Hannah broke from them nodding and pointing and rushing to Avigail. James stared at me, at her, and me again, and then, his face stricken with grief, he bowed his head.

"No, stop it, all of you, get back," I said as I came forward, passing her, and standing in front of her. Silent Hannah stopped in her tracks. She stared at me, and then back at the crowd. In an instant she seemed to realize what she'd done.

And I realized it as well. She'd sounded the alarm that Avigail had run away. She'd brought them here, and only now did she realize her terrible mistake.

Behind me Avigail murmured a strangled prayer.

More and more men were coming, it seemed from everywhere, out of the fields, from the village, from the far road. Boys were running towards us.

Up from the village came Jason striding with Reuben of Cana beside him.

Someone shouted for the Rabbi. Everyone was shouting for the Rabbi.

James turned and shouted to his sons to get Joseph and the elders this very instant. The name "Shemayah" was bursting from everyone's lips, and suddenly Avigail ran towards me, and in a gesture as fatal as that of Yitra when he had reached for the Orphan, she flung herself against me with both arms.

Stones whizzed through the air, one narrowly missing my ear. Cries of "Hypocrite" and "Harlot" let fly along with the stones.

I turned and sheltered Avigail. James rushed forward and stood in front of us, his arm outstretched. My aunt Esther had arrived with a group of women streaming behind her and she ran forward now as well. She screamed as she backed up into us. The stones stopped.

"Shemayah, Shemayah!" men chanted, even as the crowd broke open to disgorge the Rabbi and Hananel of Cana and two of the elders at their side.

Astonished, the Rabbi looked at us, his eyes moving over every detail of the scene he beheld. I stepped forward, all but shoving James out of my path.

"I tell you, nothing has happened here, but words, words spoken together in quiet there in the grove where I come, where everyone knows that I come!"

"Avigail, do you accuse this man!" cried the Rabbi, his face white with shock.

She shook her head violently. She gasped. "No," she cried. "No, he's innocent. No, he did nothing."

"Then what is this madness!" cried the Rabbi. He turned on the crowd which was now tripling in size, and full of gawking necks and raucous demands to see and to know. "I tell you stop this now and go back down to your homes."

"Go back at once, all of you," cried Jason. "There is nothing to see here. Get away from this place. You're drunken, all of you, with your celebrations! Go home."

But murmurs and grumbling ran rampant in all directions. "Alone, in the grove together, Yeshua and Avigail." I caught it in bits and fragments. I saw Joseph hurrying up the slope. Menachim was all but carrying him. More and more women were running towards us. Avigail had broken into helpless gasping cries.

"Bring her home, now, bring her," I said. But suddenly my brother Joses had his arms around me from the back, and my brother Joseph did too.

"Don't! Stop this," I said.

"Shemayah," Joses said, and there the man was, striding up the hill, parting the crowd, shoving people out of his path.

At the sight of him, Avigail buckled. My aunt Esther tried to hold her, but Avigail doubled over and stumbled backwards and slipped out of Esther's hands.

The Rabbi stepped into Shemayah's path. Shemayah went to strike him, and the farmhands caught his upraised arm. Men seized Jason before he could strike Shemayah, and others grabbed hold of Reuben. It seemed all strove one with the other.

Shemayah threw off those who held him. He glared at his daughter and at me.

He ran at me.

"You'll drink from that broken cup for the rest of your life, you will!" Shemayah cursed. "You filthy cheating liar, you damnable thief."

Avigail shrieked. "No, stop it, he didn't . . . he did nothing!" She stood up, arms out to him. "Father, he did nothing."

"A curse on you," Shemayah shouted at me. My brothers rose up in front of him, blocking him and pushing me backwards. I felt my aunt Salome's arms around me and then the arms of my cousins Silas and Levi.

"Let me go, stop," I declared, but there were too many of them.

"You think my daughter is a harlot that you can do this to her?" Shemayah shouted, straining against the men who held him, his face red.

Over the arms that held me, I could just make out his advancing on Avigail, and grabbing her by the shoulders and shaking her so that her head fell back and her veil fell off.

A huge huzzah rose from the crowd, so loud it brought everyone to silence.

Avigail's dark mantle had fallen open. All could see the white gauze of her gold-trimmed gown. Shemayah saw it. Shemayah ripped the mantle from her and flung it to the side.

The shock of the crowd found one huge wordless voice.

Avigail stood horrified, unable to grasp what had happened. Then she looked down at herself, saw for herself what they saw: the frail, gauzy white wedding tunic, embroidered at the sleeves and hem in gold.

Silent Hannah and Shabi grabbed at Avigail's mantle and tried to give it back to her. Shemayah knocked Shabi flat on his back on the grass with his fist.

Avigail stared up at her father. She clutched at the neck of her gown, at the loose strings of gold that had been untied when she came to me, and then suddenly, she let out a low terrible cry.

"Harlot, am I?" she screamed. "Harlot! In my mother's wedding tunic, I am a harlot!"

"Stop her, get her!" I called out. "Rabbi, this is a child."

"Harlot!" she screamed again and then she tore at the neck of her gown. "I am a harlot, yes, I am a harlot, I am your harlot," she sobbed. She staggered backwards free of her father. Free of the children.

"No," I shouted. "Avigail, stop this. Rabbi! Stop this."

Jason struggled, ran forward, and was thrown to the ground by men around him.

Again came that horrid sound, the sound of stones flying. The children screamed in terror. Silent Hannah fell to the ground.

"No, stop this in the name of Heaven!" I cried.

Avigail stepped back again, screaming louder. "Harlot!" she cried. With her own hands like uplifted claws, she tore at her own hair, disheveling it and bringing it down around her face. "Look on this harlot!" she shrieked.

The chorus of judgment rose in frantic and furious shouts and cries. Stones flew past us from everywhere. I fought with all my strength against my brothers as they dragged me to the ground. I felt hands around my knees and my ankles. Struggling, panting, shouting, I was being dragged away.

The shrieking and wailing of the children cut through the hoarse curses and execrations.

"Lord God in Heaven, this cannot happen!" I cried. "Stop this!"

Father, send the rain!

A deafening crack of thunder broke overhead.

The sky darkened, the light dying in front of my eyes as I fell forward onto the stony earth and scrambled to my knees. On came the thunder again, immense and rolling. I stood on my feet. I looked up at the heavy, leaden, gathering clouds.

A knife of lightning blinded me. The crowd gasped with one voice again. The thunder crackled and bore down again.

I saw, before me on the slope, Avigail still standing, Avigail, surrounded by the children, saved by the children—by Isaac and Shabi and Yaqim and Silent Hannah, all of whom clung to her along with countless others, some of them lying at her feet, their sobbing faces turning from her to their petrified parents and from their parents to the boiling sky. My aunt Esther clung to Avigail, her arms over Avigail's head. James rose from the ground, loosed by those who'd held him, and stared stunned at the Heavens.

"Saved," I whispered. I breathed the warm wet wind. *Saved.* I closed my eyes and fell down on my knees.

The windows of Heaven opened.

The rain came pouring down.

15

It was a rain so dense and swift it brought the twilight with it, closing up the world in front of men's eyes. James and Esther picked up Avigail, off her feet, that I could see, and James slung her up high over his shoulder, the better to carry her, and all ran for the village or what shelter perhaps that they could find.

With my brothers, I took hold of Joseph, and we hoisted him to our shoulders and rushed down the hill.

We were soaked to the skin before we reached the street, and the street was a running river. Now we had the faintest lanterns to guide us through the shadows, the tramp of feet all around us, people uttering fearful cries now and bits of prayer.

But nothing could prevent us from gaining our courtyard, throwing open the doors of the house, and rushing one and all inside.

Joseph was set down gently and at once, his white hair plastered to his pink scalp. Lamp after lamp was lighted.

The women in a flock carried Avigail deep into the house, her sobs echoing off the walls, and up the stairs into the small rooms of the second floor which belonged to the women alone.

The men fell down exhausted on all sides.

Old Bruria and my mother came with dry robes for us, and together with Little Mary and Mara, who had been with them all the while, went to drying us off, taking our wet clothes, patting down our hair.

James lay back, out of breath, staring at the ceiling. I slumped against the wall.

Old Uncle Alphaeus came in, bewildered and amazed. Then Uncle Cleopas appeared from the outside, dripping and out of breath. The last of the children came in with him. It was he, along with Menachim, who bolted the door.

The rain slammed onto the tile roofs. It rushed in the gutters and down the pipes to the cisterns, and to the mikvah, and to the many jugs beneath the downspouts all round and about the house. It clattered against the wooden shutters. It crashed in gust after gust against the rattling doors.

No one spoke as we rubbed ourselves dry and put on the fresh robes given us. My mother tended to Joseph, gently peeling off the soaked garments. The children heaped up the coals, and went this way and that in their excitement, searching for even more lamps to be lighted in this dense and snug and safe place.

Suddenly there was a crashing fist against the door.

"If he dares," said James, rising to his feet with his hand out. "If he dares come here, I'll kill him."

"Hush, stop it," cried his wife, Mara.

The knock came again, measured, insistent.

A voice came from beyond the paneled wood.

I went to the door and lifted the latch and opened it.

There stood Reuben in his fine linen robes as wet through and through as anyone, and his father, bent beneath a covering of soaked wool, and behind them their horses and their hired men.

James immediately welcomed them into the house.

I went with the hired men and the animals to the stables. The door hadn't been shut. The place was wet, but we soon had the horses unharnessed, and a fresh layer of hay on the ground. The men gestured in thanks. They had their wine, they held up the skins, and told me to go on.

I edged back to the main door, under the overhang, but I was still wet when I came into the house.

Again, my mother greeted me with a dry mantle and I stood against the door, breathing deeply, and catching my breath.

Hananel and his grandson, dressed in fresh dry wool, sat beside the low brazier, opposite Joseph. All had cups of wine in their hands. Joseph gave the blessing now in a hushed voice and bid the guests drink.

The old scholar looked up at me and then to Joseph. Then he tasted the wine and set it down before his crossed ankles.

"Who speaks for the girl now?" he asked.

"Grandfather, please . . ." Reuben said. "I thank you all for your kindness, thank you."

"Who speaks for her?" demanded Hananel. "I won't stay in this miserable town one moment longer than is necessary. For this I came, and on this I now speak."

Joseph gestured to James.

"I speak for her," said James. "My father and I speak for her. And what is it you want to say to me on her account? The girl's our kinswoman."

"Ah, and ours as well," said Hananel. "What do you think I want to say? Why do you think I dragged myself through this downpour? I came here this day with an offer of marriage for the girl on behalf of my grandson, Reuben, who sits here to my right, and who is well known to you, as I am known to you. And I speak now of marriage for my son and this girl. Her evil father has abandoned her before the elders of this village and in plain sight of everyone present, including myself and my grandson, and so if you speak for her, then speak for her now to me."

Joseph laughed.

No one else said a word, or moved, or even breathed very deeply. But Joseph laughed. He looked at the ceiling. His hair was dried now and very white and his eyes were moist in the glimmer from the coals. He laughed as if he was dreaming.

"Ah, Hananel," he said. "How I have missed you, and I didn't even know it."

"Yes, and I've missed you too, Joseph," said Hananel. "Now before any of you clever men say so, allow me to say so: the girl is innocent; she was innocent yesterday; she is innocent today. And the girl is very young."

"Amen," I said.

"But she's not poor," said James without missing a heartbeat. "She has her money from her mother, and she'll have a proper marriage contract hammered out here in this room before she'll be betrothed to anyone or married to anyone, and she will be a bride from this door on her wedding night."

Hananel nodded. "Get the ink and the parchment," he said. "Ah, listen to this rain. What chance is there that I'll sleep under my own roof tonight?"

"You're welcome to sleep under our roof, my lord," I said, with James murmuring his fierce assent. Everyone took it up, the welcomes. My mother and Old Bruria were setting out pottage for us, and warm bread.

From somewhere deep in the house, somewhere above the first story, I could hear the murmur of women's voices. Even beneath the constant hammer of the rain. I saw Mara come back in when I had not even seen her go out. So Avigail knew of all this, my precious and anguished Avigail.

Aunt Esther brought the parchment, several loose sheets, and the ink and the pen.

"Write it up, write it all up," said Hananel airily. "Write up that everything pertaining to her inheritance from her mother is hers, according to every record public, private, written, and unwritten, known to tradition and unrecorded except by common consent, or according to the girl's own avowal, and in spite of the denials of her father. Write it up."

"My lord," my mother said. "This is all we have to offer you, I fear, only a little pottage but the bread is fresh and just warmed."

"It's a banquet, my child," he said, bowing his head gravely. "I knew your father and loved him. This is good bread." He beamed up at her, and then glared at James. "And what are you writing?"

"Why, I'm writing just exactly what you said."

And so it began.

It lasted an hour.

They talked, back and forth, of all the usual conditions and proprieties. James haggled mercilessly over every single point. The girl's property was hers in perpetuity and should her husband ever, no matter what anyone said, put her aside, her property would be returned to her and with such damages as her kinsmen would demand, and so forth and so on, as it was always done, back and forth, back and forth. Yet James drove every point home. Now and then Cleopas gave him a nod, or held up a cautious finger, but in general it was James who saw to it, until it was written out. And signed.

"Now, I beg you, my lords, to allow this bride to be married immediately," declared Hananel with a weary shrug. His voice was slurred now from the wine, and he pinched his nose as if his eyes ached. "In view of what the child has suffered, in view of the disposition of her father, let this happen at once. In three days' time or sooner, I insist, for the girl's sake. I will immediately seek to prepare my house."

"No, my lord," I said. "That won't do."

James gave me a sharp look, full of apprehension and distrust. But not a single woman in the room looked at me. It was plain enough to them what I meant when I spoke.

"In several months' time," I said, "at Purim, Avigail will be ready for the bridegroom to come for her at this threshold, properly arrayed for her new husband and beneath the canopy, with all our kinsmen to salute you and sing for you, and proceed with you and dance with you, and she will then be yours."

James stared at me wrathfully. My uncle raised his eyebrows but didn't speak. Joseph watched in quiet.

But my mother nodded. The other women nodded.

"That's over three months' time," Reuben said with a sigh.

"Yes, my lord," I said. "And right after Purim, after we've all heard the Scroll of Esther, as we should."

Hananel studied me, and then nodded. "This is good. We are agreed."

"But now, if I might," asked Reuben. "If I might for just a moment see the girl, speak to her, present to her this gift."

"What is this gift?" demanded James.

I motioned for him to back off. Everybody knew the betrothal wouldn't be final until Avigail had received Reuben's gift.

James stared at Reuben sullenly.

Reuben produced the gift dutifully, opening the silken wrapping. It was a gold necklace, very delicate and very beautifully made. It shone with gems. I'd seldom seen such a thing. It might have come from Babylon or from Rome.

"Let me see if the girl is well and able to speak to you," said my mother. "My lord, drink your wine, and give me leave to talk to her. I'll be back as soon as I can."

There were muffled noises from the room next to us. Several of the women came in. Reuben rose and so did James. I was already standing.

Hananel looked up expectantly, the light very bright on his slightly scornful and bored face.

Avigail was brought in the door.

She was dressed in a simple bleached woolen tunic and robe, and her hair was beautifully combed.

The women urged her gently forward. Reuben stood before her.

He whispered her name. He held out the silk-wrapped gift with both hands as though it was something fragile that might shatter. "For you, my bride," he said. "If you will accept."

Avigail looked up at me. I nodded.

"Go on, you may accept it," said James.

Avigail received the present and opened the silk. She stared at the necklace. She was silent. She was dazed.

Her eyes locked on those of Reuben of Cana.

I looked down at the grandfather's face. He was transformed. The cold hard look of scorn was broken and dissolved. He stared up at Avigail and his grandson. He said nothing.

It was Reuben who spoke in a halting voice.

"My precious Avigail," he said. "I've traveled many a mile since I last saw you. I've seen many a wonder and studied in many a school, and wandered to many a place. But through it all, I carried in my heart one most cherished memory with me, and that was of you, Avigail, of you as you sang with the maidens on the road to Jerusalem. And in my dreams, I heard your voice."

They stared at one another. Avigail's face was smooth, and her eyes soft and large. Then Reuben flushed red and hastily reached for the necklace, slipping it out of the silk in her hands which fluttered to the ground. He opened the clasp and he gestured: Might he put it around her neck?

"Yes," said my mother.

And my mother took the necklace from him and she closed the clasp at the back of Avigail's neck.

I stepped up and put my hands on the shoulders of Reuben and Avigail.

"Speak to the young man, Avigail," I said softly. "Let him know what's in your heart."

Avigail's face softened and heated and her voice came low and full of emotion.

"I am happy, Reuben." Then her eyes melted. "I've suffered misfortune," she whispered.

"I know this. . . ."

"I haven't been wise!"

"Avigail," I whispered. "You are to be a bride now."

"My young one," Reuben said. "Who of us is wise in such adversity? What is youth and what is innocence, but treasures that we're soon to lose in the world's trials? That the Good Lord has preserved you for me through my years of foolish roaming, I can give only thanks."

The women surrounded them, hugging them and patting them, and then they drew Reuben back, and they took Avigail away, to the far end of the house and up the steps.

I looked at Hananel. He was staring at me fixedly. His eyes were cunning, but his look was chastened and faintly sad.

It seemed everyone was on the move now in the room, urging our guests to make ready, if they wanted, for bed in a clean, dry room which had been readied for them, or insisting that they take more wine, or that they have more food, or rest, or whatever it was in the world they should desire.

Hananel kept his eyes on me. He reached up for me. I came round and sat down beside him.

"My lord?" I asked.

"Thank you, Yeshua bar Joseph," he said, "that you came to my house."

16

AT LAST OUR GUESTS were securely bedded down in their rooms, on the best rugs we had laid over straw for beds, with the few fine pillows we could gather, and the inevitable brazier of coals, and water should they require it. Of course they claimed it was more than they had ever expected, and we knew it was not, and insisted that we wished we could provide them with silken bedding, and they urged us to go on to sleep, and I came back to the main room where I almost always slept and fell down beside the brazier.

Joseph sat silent as before, gazing at me with thoughtful eyes, and Uncle Cleopas sat staring at the fire and savoring the cup of his wine, sipping from it, murmuring to himself.

I knew a wrenching misery. I knew it as I lay still in the silence and in the shadows, ignoring the coming and settling of my brothers Joseph and Judas. I knew it as vaguely as I was aware that Silas and Levi were there too and Little Cleopas with his wife, Mary.

I knew that Avigail was saved; I knew that somehow her misery was at an end. I knew that Hananel and his grandson Reuben would be good to her all her days. I knew that.

But I also knew that I had given Avigail away to another man, I'd given Avigail away forever.

And a wealth of possibilities now descended on me, possibilities which I'd glimpsed perhaps in the heated moments in the grove when I'd clung to her, possibilities choked off by necessity and decision. Now they came like the whispered taunts given an airy shape passing before my dulled eyes— Avigail, my wife, Avigail and I together with a house of little ones, Avigail and I amid trivial tasks and arbors of trailing vines, in weariness and with soft tender skin, dare one think of that, the brush of lips, yes, and a body crooked snugly against me in the night-to-night dark—ah, the essence of all that would have followed, and could have followed, if I'd taken her as my wife, if I'd done what every man in the village expected of me, what my brothers had expected of me long before the other men, if I'd done what custom and tradition required of me. If I'd done what my heart seemed to want from me.

I didn't want sleep. I feared sleep. I wanted peace, I wanted the day to come so I could walk, I wanted the rain to keep falling so that it would blot out every sound in this room, every spoken word. And why at all at this hour and after so much were they speaking?

I looked up. James stood glowering at me. Beside him stood Cleopas. My mother stood there trying to pull her brother away, and finally James let it out:

"And how are we to provide this bride with proper robes and veils and a canopy and all the attendants of which you so vehemently spoke, to marry such a man as the grandson of Hananel of Cana!" He rose off the balls of his feet in rage. "Tell me, what is it that lies behind your boast, you, who caused this disaster, this very disaster. How could you claim for her a raiment and preparations such as no one in this house could ever give to your sister!"

There was a flood of words yet to come.

But I rose to my feet.

My uncle Cleopas spoke gently. "Why couldn't you have married her yourself, my son?" he asked pleadingly. "Who is it that asks this of you, that you don't marry?"

"Oh, he's too good for that," declared James. "He would do Moses one better and not take a wife; he would do Elijah better and not take a wife. He would live as an Essene but not with the Essenes for he's too good for them. And had it been any other man in that grove with the girl, she'd be ruined. But all know you, no, you would never have touched her."

He drew in his breath for another rush of words, but I stopped him.

"Before you make yourself positively ill with rage," I said, "let me ask my mother—bring here, please now, the gifts that were given to me when I was born. Set them here before us."

"My son, are you certain?"

"I am certain," I said. I kept my eye on James.

He went to speak and I said:

"Wait."

She went out directly.

James stood regarding me with cold contempt, ready at any moment to erupt. My brothers were now grouped about, behind him. My nephews stood watching, and into the room had come Aunt Esther and Mara. Shabi and Isaac and Menachim stood against the wall.

I looked unwaveringly at James.

"I am weary of you, my brother," I said. "In my heart, I'm weary."

He narrowed his eyes. He was astonished.

My mother came back. She held a chest which was heavy for her to hold, and Mara and Esther assisted her as she brought it forward and set it down on the floor in front of us.

Decades, it had been hidden away, this chest, ever since our return here from Egypt. James had seen this chest. James knew what it was, but my other brothers had never set eyes on it, as they were the sons of my uncle Cleopas, and they'd been born after me. None of the younger men had ever seen it. Perhaps the boys in the room had never even heard tell of it. Perhaps Mara and Little Mary didn't even know that it existed.

It was a Persian chest, plated in gold and exquisitely decorated with curling vines and pomegranates. Even the handles of the chest were gold. It shone in the light, brilliantly as the gold of Avigail's necklace had shone on her neck.

"It's never enough for you, is it, James!" I said. My voice was low. I struggled against my anger. "Not the angels filling up the night skies over Bethlehem, not the shepherds who came through the stable door to tell my mother and father of the angels' song, no, not enough for you. And not the Magi themselves, the richly clad men from Persia who descended on the narrow streets of Bethlehem with their caravan, brought there by a star that lighted the very Heavens. Not enough for you! Not enough for you that you yourself saw these men put this chest at the foot of my cradle. No, not enough, never enough, no sign ever. Not the words of our blessed cousin Elizabeth, mother of John bar Zechariah, before she died—when she told us all of the words spoken by her husband as he named his son, John, when she told us of the angel who'd come to him. No, not enough. Not even the words of the prophets."

I stopped. He was frightened. He backed away and my brothers shifted uneasily away from me.

I stepped forward and James stepped back again.

"Well, you are my older brother," I said, "and you are the head of this family, and I owe you obedience, and I owe you patience. And obedience I have tendered and patience I have tried, and will try again, and, with it all, respect for you, whom I love and have always loved, knowing who you are and what you are, and what you've endured and what we all must endure."

He was speechless and shaken.

"But now," I said. "Now hear this." I reached down and opened the chest. I threw the lid back. I stared at the contents, the glistening alabaster jars, and the great collection of gold coins that it held, nestled in their tapestried box. I lifted the box. I emptied the coins onto the floor. I saw them glittering as they scattered.

"Now hear this," I said. "This is mine, and was given me at my birth, and I give it now for Avigail's bridal raiment, and for her rings, and for her bracelets and for all the wealth that's been taken from her; I give it for her canopy. I give it for her! And my brother, I tell you now I will not marry. And this—this is my ransom from it!" I pointed to the coins. "My ransom!"

Helplessly, he looked at me. He looked at the scattered coins. Persian coins. Pure gold. The purest gold of which a man can form a coin.

I didn't look down at them again. I'd seen them once long ago. I knew what they looked like; I knew how they felt, what they weighed. I didn't look now. But I saw them shining in the darkness.

My vision was blurred as I looked at James.

"I love you, my brother," I said. "Let me in peace now!"

His hands hovered, fingers opening uncertainly. He reached out for me.

We stood reaching for each other.

But a knock sounded on the door, an insistent knock, and after it another and another.

From without came the loud voice of Jason. "Yeshua, open to us. Yeshua, open now."

I hung my head and folded my arms. I looked at my mother and gave her the most weary smile and she clasped my neck with her hand.

Cleopas opened the door.

In, from the crashing downpour, came the Rabbi, under a tent of wool wrappings, and with him Jason, covered in the same way. The door banged in the wind, and the wind gusted through the room, like a beast let loose among us. Cleopas shut the door.

"Yeshua," said the Rabbi without a word to anyone else standing. "In the name of Heaven, stop it."

"Stop it?" asked James. "Stop what!"

"The rain, Yeshua!" said the Rabbi earnestly, imploring me, from beneath his shadow hood of wool. "Yeshua, it's an inundation!"

"Yeshua," said Jason, "the village is going to be washed away. Every cistern, mikvah, jug is full. We're in a lake! Will you look outside? Will you listen to it? Can't you hear it?"

"You want me to pray for it to stop?" I asked.

"Yes," said the Rabbi. "You prayed for it to start, didn't you?"

"I prayed for weeks as did everyone else," I said. That was true. Then my thoughts returned to the terrible moment on the open slope. *Father, stop this . . . send the rain.* "Rabbi," I said. "Whatever I prayed, it was the Lord Himself who sent the rain to us."

"Well, that is so, most certainly, my son," said the Rabbi soothingly, his hands out to clasp mine. "But will you please pray now for the Lord to make the rain stop! I beg you."

My aunt Esther began to laugh. Slowly Cleopas began to laugh too, but this was low whispering laughter, this, until my aunt Salome joined in, and then Little Mary.

"Silence!" said James. He was still shaking from all that

had gone before, but he collected himself, and looked to me. "Yeshua, will you lead us in prayer that the Lord will close up the windows of Heaven now, if it's His will?"

"Get on with it!" declared Jason.

"Be still," said the Rabbi. "Yeshua, pray."

I bowed my head. I put them all far from my mind. I cleared my mind of anything that could stand between me and the words I spoke; I put my heart and my breath into them.

"Merciful Lord, Creator of all good things," I said, "who saved us this day from spilling innocent—."

"Yeshua! Just pray for it to stop!" Jason cried. "Otherwise every member of this family might as well grab hammer and nails and wood and start building an ark outside because we will all need it!"

Cleopas dissolved into irresistible laughter. The women were muffling their smiles. The children stared aghast.

"May I continue?"

"Pray do before every house melts to ruin," said Jason.

"Lord in Heaven, if it is Your will, bring this rain to an end."

The rain stopped.

The pummeling of the roof stopped. The gusting clatter against the shutters stopped. The high whistling sound of the rain hitting the flags outside was gone.

The room was wrapped in uneasy silence. And there came the gurgling of the water running still in the gutters, finding its way down the many pipes, dripping and splashing from the overhangs.

A coolness came over me, a prickling sensation, as if my skin were doubly alive. I felt an emptiness, and then a gradual replenishing of whatever had gone out of me. I sighed, and once again my vision was moist and blurred.

I heard the Rabbi intoning the psalm of thanks. I said the words along with him.

When he had reached the last word, I took up another in the sacred tongue:

" 'Let the sea and what fills it resound,' " I said, " 'and the world and those who dwell in it. Let the rivers clap their hands, the mountains cry out with them in joy, before the Lord who comes, who comes to govern the earth, to govern the world with justice and the peoples with fairness.' "

They said it along with me.

I was dizzy now and so tired that I could have dropped where I was. I turned and reached for the wall, and slowly sat down to the left of the brazier. Joseph sat watching as before.

Finally I looked up. All stood quiet, including the littlest children in the room. The Rabbi was peering down at me gently and wistfully and Jason was marveling.

Then Jason snapped to wakefulness and said with a bow, "Thank you, Yeshua."

The Rabbi added his thanks, and so did the others present, one by one.

Then Jason pointed.

"Ah, what is that!" He stared at the gold chest. His eyes moved over the scattered coins that glinted in the dimness.

He gasped with amazement. "So that's the treasure," he said. "Why, I never really believed it."

"Come, let's go," said the Rabbi, pushing him towards the door. "A good night to you, blessed children, and blessings on all under this roof, and again, we thank you."

Back and forth came the polite whispers, offers of wine, the inevitable demurring, the door opening and closing. The silence. I fell over on my side, my arm for a pillow, and I closed my eyes.

Someone picked up the coins, and put them back in their case. That much I heard. Soft shuffling steps. And then I was drifting downwards, into a safe place, a place where I could be for a little while alone, no matter how many were gathered around me.

17

THE LAND WAS WASHED CLEAN. The creek was brimming and the fields had soaked up the rain and were soon fit for plowing, with time still for a bountiful harvest. The dust no longer choked the living grass and the ancient trees, and the roads though soft and spongy on the first day were by the second quite fine, and all over the unplanted hills there sprang up the inevitable, faithful wildflowers.

Every cistern, mikvah, jug, pitcher, bucket, and barrel in Nazareth and the surrounding towns had been filled with water. And the town bustled with those washing clothing in luxury and gladness. The women went to work with renewed passion in the kitchen gardens.

Of course legend told of many a holy man who could make rain come, and make rain stop, if only he appealed to the Lord, the most famous of which was probably Honi, the Circle Drawer, a Galilean of generations past, but there had been many another.

And so people rushed up to me as I went in and out, not to say, Ah, what a miracle, Yeshua, but rather "Why didn't you pray for the rain to come sooner?" or "Yeshua, we knew if only you would pray, but the question is why did you wait so long," and so forth and so on.

Some of this was said in jesting, most in very bold goodwill. But some made these remarks with a sneer, and in my hearing there was plenty of murmuring, at work and in Nazareth, of "Had it been any other man in that grove!" and "Well, you know it was Yeshua, of course, nothing happened."

The family was all astir with the work that needed to be done, and even Silent Hannah was pressed to leave the village for the first time since her arrival years before, and go with my aunts and my mother into Sepphoris, there to get the finest sheer linen for Avigail's tunic, and robes and veils, and to find those who sell or sew the most intricate of gold-threaded needlework.

As we worked on our various jobs in Sepphoris, I found every reason I could to assist James, and he took the little kindnesses from me graciously. I put my arm around him whenever I could, and he turned and did this with me; and our brothers saw these embraces, and heard the easy words, and so did the women at home. Indeed his wife, Mara, said that he seemed something of a new man and she wished I'd dressed him down a long time ago. But that she didn't say to me. I heard it from my aunt Esther in a whisper.

Of course James asked at some point, because he thought it best, should someone send for the midwife again to put the mind of Reuben of Cana at rest? I thought my aunts would destroy him with their bare hands.

"And how many midwives can wander in that virgin territory," demanded my aunt Esther, "before they break down the very door they're seeking to find intact, do you think?"

And that was the end of that subject.

Avigail I never saw. She was deeply secluded with Old Bruria in rooms to which only the women went, but three letters had come for her from Reuben bar Daniel bar Hananel of Cana, and she'd read them out to all assembled and written her replies in her own hand, gentle and sweet sentiments, and these letters I myself took for her to Cana.

As for Reuben, he was in the village every chance he got with Jason disputing this or that point of the law, but mostly hanging about in the vain hopes of catching a glimpse of his bride which was not to happen.

As for Shemayah, his shame was erased. A rich man, far richer than any in Nazareth, had done what a poor man might dream of doing, and those in between might never attempt. And this had been done swiftly and completely.

The first anyone heard of Shemayah was a week later when he heaved into our courtyard every single item or article of clothing that had ever belonged to his daughter, Avigail.

Oh, well, these precious things were in leather chests, and no worse for having come crashing through the lattice like so many missiles hurled at a besieged city.

As for myself, I was in torment.

I was as weary as a man who'd trudged for seven days without cease up a sheer mountain. I couldn't go to the grove to sleep. No, the grove was now tainted by my own blunders and I would never have that peace again, not without bringing forth fresh recriminations and scowls and scorn. The grove was forfeit.

And never had I so needed it. Never had I so needed to be alone, pleasing as it was to be amid such frank and innocent happiness.

I walked.

I walked at evening through the hills; I walked to Cana and back and walked as far as I could and sometimes made my way home under heavy darkness, my mantle wrapped tight around me, my fingers freezing. I didn't care how cold I was. I didn't care how tired I was. I had one purpose and that was to wear myself out so that I could sleep without dreams, and thereby somehow endure the pain I felt.

I could put no real finger on this pain. It wasn't that men whispered as to my having been alone with the girl; it wasn't that I would soon see her happily married. It wasn't even that I had wounded my brother, because in the healing of that wound, I felt his warm love for me and mine for him all the more keenly.

It was a terrible restlessness, a sense again that all that happened around me was somehow a sign to me.

At last one afternoon after the work of the day was done—the laying of a floor, in fact, which had hurt my knees about as badly as it ever did—I went to the House of the Essenes in Sepphoris, and let their gentle linen-clad men wash my feet as they did for any weary man who wandered in, and I let them give me a cold drink of water.

I sat in a small foyer near the courtyard watching them for a long time. I wasn't sure of the names of those who worked at this house. The Essenes had many such houses, though not of course for men such as myself, who lived only a few miles away, but for travelers in need of lodgings.

Did they know me, these young men, who had come from other communities of the Essenes? I didn't know. I searched the shifting groups of those who swept and cleaned and, even beyond, those reading in the small library. There were old ones here, old ones who no doubt knew everyone.

I didn't dare to shape a question in my mind. I only sat there, waiting. Waiting.

Finally one of the very old men, swaying as he made his way to me with one leg dragging and his right hand knotted on a stick, came and sat on the bench beside me.

"Yeshua bar Joseph," he said, "have you heard any word at all of late from your cousin?"

That was the answer to my question.

They didn't know where John bar Zechariah was, any more than we did.

I admitted that we'd had no word, and we talked then in quiet, the old man and I, about those who go off into the wilderness to pray, to be alone with the Lord, and what it must be like, those lonely nights under the stars with the howling desert wind. The old man himself did not know. I did not know. John's name was not spoken again, by either one of us.

At last, I went home, taking the longest routes, up this little hillock and down through that olive glade and up past the creek and through it and on until I was bone weary and glad to fall down by the fire, and could without effort look truly too forlorn for anyone to question me.

How many days passed?

I didn't count them. The rain visited us again in light and beautiful showers. A blessing for every blade of grass in the fields.

Shemayah was seen back at work, with the hands who'd gone ahead with the plowing when he himself had remained indoors refusing to give the simplest orders. I saw him one morning, barreling through the street and crashing into his own door as if to make war on his own household.

Days. Days of bracing cold, and gliding white clouds, and the earth vibrantly green all around us. Days of the ivy climbing the lattices once more, and days of happy designs and happy hopes. Little Cleopas and Little Mary would soon have a child, or so I was told, though of course I'd seen the evidence of it. And nothing new from Judea except that Pontius Pilate, the Governor, seemed to have settled in with only a few minor disputes with the Temple authorities.

One night after deliberately roaming until I could roam

no more, my head teeming, I trudged in, well after supper, ate a piece of bread and pottage, and went to sleep. I felt my mother put a clean fresh-smelling blanket over me. With the water now so plentiful the house smelled of freshly washed wool. I kissed her hand before she withdrew. I went through the layers of dreams and softly into nothingness.

Suddenly I awoke. I'd been with someone who'd been weeping. Terrible weeping. The weeping of a man who can't weep. The suffocated and desperate weeping of someone who cannot bear to do it.

All was well in the room. The women sewed by the fire. My mother asked, "What is it?"

"Weeping," I said. "Someone crying."

"Not in this house," said James.

I pushed off the blanket. "Where is the marriage contract for Avigail?"

"What, safely in that chest, why do you ask?" said James. "What's the matter with you?"

This was not the golden chest of the Magi's gifts. This was the simple chest in which we kept our ink and our important papers.

I went to the chest, opened it, and took out the marriage contract. I rolled it up tight, slipped a loose scrap of soft leather around it, and went out.

A faint bit of rain had fallen earlier.

The streets were shimmering. Nazareth under the luminous Heavens looked like a town made of silver.

The door of Shemayah's house was open. The barest light escaped.

I went to the door. I pushed it back.

I heard him crying. I heard that awful choking sound, that bitter sound almost as if he were strangling in his pain.

He sat alone in a cheerless room. The coals had long ago

died to ash. One lamp burnt there, on the floor, a little crockery lamp, and the oil was faintly scented—the only comfort at all here.

I shut the door, and came and sat beside him. He didn't look at me.

I knew how this had to begin, and so I told him how sorry I was for all I'd done that had made him so miserable. I confessed.

"I am so sorry, Shemayah," I said.

His cries grew loud. They grew huge in the little room. But he had no words. He slumped forward. He rocked back and forth.

"Shemayah, I have here the contract for her marriage," I said. "It's all done properly and right, and she'll be married to Reuben of Cana. It's here, Shemayah, it's written."

He groped with his left hand, gently batting at the paper, gently pushing the contract away, and then he turned blindly to me, and I felt his heavy arm go around my neck. He wept on my shoulder.

18

IT WAS AN HOUR perhaps before I left him. I brought back the marriage contract and put it in the chest. No one noticed.

Jason was there, and the Rabbi—they were on their feet and so were most of my brothers—and they were all talking excitedly.

"Where have you been!" cried my mother, and then it seemed I was surrounded by anxious faces. There was the rustling of parchment, Jason shaking my shoulder.

"Jason, let me be tonight, please," I said. "I'm sleepy, and I want nothing but to go to bed. Whatever it is, can't we talk about this tomorrow?"

"Oh, but you must hear this," said my mother. "Little Mary," she said. "Go, call Avigail."

I started to ask what I must hear, what was so important that Avigail should be woken up and brought in, but they told me all at once in broken phrases.

"Letters," said my mother. "Letters you must hear."

"Letters," said the Rabbi, "letters from Capernaum, from your cousin, John bar Zebedee, and from your sister, Little Salome."

"The rider just brought the mail," Jason declared. "I have

a letter. My uncle has a letter. Letters have come to people up one side of the hill and down the other. Listen, you must hear all this. By tomorrow and the next day, all Galilee will know these things."

I sank down in my usual corner.

Joseph was awake, seated straight against the wall, watching the others keenly.

"This news is from Jerusalem," said Jason, "and the letter to my uncle, it's from Tiberias."

Avigail, sleepy and concerned, had come into the room and sat down with Little Mary.

James held up his letter for me to see. "From John bar Zebedee, our cousin," he said. "And this is for all of us . . . and for you."

The Rabbi turned, and took the letter from James.

"Please, James," he said, "may I read it because he is the one who's seen these things, your young cousin."

James at once gave the letter over to him. Joses handed James the lamp and he held it high so the Rabbi could read by the light of it.

The letter was in Greek. The Rabbi hurried through the salutation:

" 'This I must make known to you all and you must give this word especially to my cousin Yeshua bar Joseph and not rest until he has heard this.

" 'Our kinsman, John bar Zechariah, has come out of the wilderness and to the Jordan and makes his way northward towards the Sea of Galilee. He is baptizing all those who are coming out to him. He is wearing only a coat of camel skin and a leather girdle, and he's lived in the wilderness on nothing but the meat of locusts and wild honey. Now he is saying to all, "I am the voice of one crying in the wilderness, Make straight the way of the Lord." And "Repent, for the Kingdom of Heaven is at hand." And all are coming to him, coming from Jerusalem and Jericho and the towns northward and down from the sea. And these he baptizes as they confess their sins. And this is what John has said to those Pharisees who've come forward to question him. "No, I am not the Christ. Nor am I the prophet. I baptize with water; but after me comes One mightier than I, whose sandals I'm not worthy to carry for Him; He will baptize you with the Holy Spirit, and with fire. He is among you, but you do not know who He is." ' " The Rabbi paused, then read on. " 'This I've seen with my own eyes, and I ask you, my kindred, again to convey these words to Yeshua bar Joseph, as I return now to the Jordan, John bar Zebedee.' "

The Rabbi lowered the stiff parchment and looked at me and at Joseph, and at Jason.

"They're going to him by the hundreds," said Jason. "From all the towns up and down the river, from the Holy City and back. The Priests and the Pharisees have gone out to him."

"But what does it mean," my uncle Cleopas asked, "that he baptizes for the forgiveness of sins? When has anyone done such a thing? Does he do this as a Priest, as was his father?"

"No," said the Rabbi. "I do not think that he does do it as a Priest." He gave the letter back to James.

"Listen to this," said Jason. "This is what he's said to the Pharisees and the Sadducees who went out from Jerusalem to question him." He read from his letter, " ' "You are a generation of vipers, and who warned you to flee from the wrath to come? Bring forth fruits of repentance before you come to me. And don't think to say to yourselves or each other, We have Abraham for our father. For I say to you that God is able to take these stones here and raise up from them sons of Abraham." ' "

Jason stopped and looked at me. He looked at Joseph and then back to the Rabbi.

My brother Joses spoke up. "But what can it mean? Is he declaring with the Essenes that the Temple is impure, that the sin offerings there don't matter?"

"He's moving now north into Perea," said Jason. "I'm going there. I want to see this new thing for myself."

"And will you be baptized? Will you do this rite for the forgiveness of sins?" asked the Rabbi softly. "Will you do this?"

"I will do it if it seems right to do it," Jason declared.

"But what can it mean, one man baptizing another, or a woman for that matter?" asked my aunt Esther. "What does it mean? Are we not all Jews? Are we not purified when we come out of the baths and enter the Temple Courts? Not even the proselytes are bathed for the forgiveness of sins, are they? Is he saying to us all that we must be proselytes?"

I stood up.

"I'm going," I said.

"We're all going with you," said Joseph. Immediately my mother said the same. All my brothers nodded.

My mother handed me the letter she had from my sister, Little Salome. My eyes fell on the words "from Bethsaida, from Capernaum."

Old Bruria spoke up. "I want to make this journey. We'll take this child with us," she said, putting her arm around Avigail.

"We will all make this journey," said James. "All of you, immediately as soon as it's light, we pack up and we go, and we take provisions as we would for the festival. We all go."

"Yes," said the Rabbi, "it's as if we were going to the Temple, going for a festival, and we will all go. Yes. I'll go with you. Now, come with me, Jason, I must talk to the elders."

"I can hear voices out there," said Menachim. "Listen. Everybody's talking about it."

He rushed out into the darkness, letting the door flap behind him.

My mother had bowed her head and placed her hand on her ear as though listening to a distant and dim voice. I drew close to her.

Jason had rushed out. The Rabbi was going. Old Bruria came up beside us.

My mother was remembering, reciting, " 'And he will be filled with the Holy Spirit even from his mother's womb. He will turn many of the children of Israel to the Lord their God. He will go before Him in the spirit and power of Elijah to turn the hearts of fathers toward children and the disobedient to the understanding of the righteous—to prepare a people fit for the Lord.' "

"But who said this?" asked Little Joseph. Shabi and Isaac clamored with the same question.

"Whose words are those?" Silas asked.

"They were spoken to another," said my mother, "but by one who also came to me." She looked up at me. Her eyes were sad.

All around us the others accosted each other with comments, questions, talk of making preparations.

"Don't be afraid," I said to my mother. I drew her near me and kissed her. I could scarcely contain my happiness.

She closed her eyes and leaned against my chest.

Suddenly amid all the haste and talk, amid the general consent that we would all go, that nothing could be done now really in the dark, that we must wait for first light, amid all this—holding tight to her, I understood the expression I'd seen in her eyes. I understood what I'd thought was fear or sadness.

And will I look back on these days, these long exhausting days, will I look back on them ever from someplace else, very far away from here, and think, Ah, these were blessed days? Will they be so tenderly remembered?

No one heard her except me as she spoke. "There was a man in the Temple when we took you there," she said, "right after you were born, before the Magi had come with their gifts."

I listened.

"And he said to me, 'And a sword shall cut through your own heart also.' "

"Ah, those words you've never told me before," I answered her, secretively, as if I were only kissing her.

"No, but I wonder if it isn't now," she said.

"This is a happy time now," I said. "This is a sweet and good time, and we are all one household as we go out. Isn't that so?"

"Yes," she whispered. "Now, let me go. I have many things to do."

"One minute longer," I said. I clung to her.

I only let her go when I had to do it. Someone was shouting that Reuben had ridden in from Cana, that he too had the news. And that Shemayah stood in the street opposite staring into our courtyard.

I knew I had to go to him, to take him by the hand, and to bring him in to see Avigail.

19

IT WAS A LONG JOURNEY EAST and south, step by step
and song by song.

By evening of the first day, we were a great shapeless mass
of pilgrims, as great as we'd ever been on the road to
Jerusalem, and indeed as many came now out of the villages
and towns for this as they would have for that.

Shemayah and all his field hands had come along with us.
But Avigail rode in the cart with my mother and my elderly
aunts, and Little Mary, all of whom seldom crowded into it
at the very same time. Joseph and Uncle Cleopas rode with
Uncle Alphaeus in the bigger cart, against the numerous
bundles and baskets, the Rabbi rode his own white donkey,
and Reuben and Jason their powerful restless horses, which
often carried them prancing ahead to wait for us at the
next town marketplace, or well, or simply to come slowly
inevitably riding back.

Old Hananel of Cana and his slaves caught up with us
on the third day, and thereafter remained with us, though we
were committed to a fairly plodding pace. And at evening it
was just like the pilgrimages with the spreading out of our
blankets, our tents, our fires, our prayers and hymns.

Everywhere we stopped we encountered those who'd

been to the river, those who'd been baptized by John and his disciples, those who'd heard "the prophet John" for themselves. An air of gaiety surrounded those returning home, a fresh sense of expectation, though it attached itself to no particular prophecy, and no particular complaint or unrest.

Of course the men never stopped demanding to know, What was this baptism? And what did it mean? Teachers and scholars joined us, young men on horseback passed us. We came upon groups of the King's soldiers who'd been to the river and had only good things to say of it, and even bands of Roman soldiers headed to the river from Caesarea stopped to share a drink of wine with us, or take a bit of pottage and bread.

The Romans were curious about this strange man drawing crowds to the riverbanks. They spoke to us a little wearily of it; yet they too wanted to see the man in camel skin who stood knee-deep in the Jordan offering a purification. After all, they said, they had their own shrines back home here and there, and their own rites, just as we did. We nodded to this. We were happy to have them sit for a while or take a morsel of food before they hurried on.

Scholars sat in circles in the evening, reciting the Scriptures as to this great matter of purifying oneself in the waters of the Jordan. They spoke of the prophet Elisha and how he had sent Naaman, the Leper, to bathe seven times in the Jordan. "But the prophet did not baptize him," one of the scholars said. "No, not himself, he did not, but told the man to bathe."

"And remember," the Rabbi said quickly one evening, "that the Leper was scornful of the prophet, was he not? Scoffing at him, yes, remember, and angry that the prophet didn't even come out to him but sent him to do this—and what, I ask you, what indeed came to pass?"

Often the subject came up: we were celebrating our

recent victory in Caesarea? The Rabbis and Pharisees spoke of this, and so did the soldiers. The Rabbis pointed out, in strong terms, that the place to give thanks to the Lord was not on the riverbank but in the Temple, the Temple which had been so grossly defiled by the approach of Pilate's ensigns. No one disagreed with this.

And when the Roman soldiers inquired, Were we having a joyful time of it because the Governor had stepped back from his position, they weren't particularly quarrelsome or concerned, only wondering, Why are so many people going to see this man, people from north and south and east and west, people even from the Greek cities of the Decapolis?

Indeed, sooner or later, almost everyone had something to say as to the sheer size of the throng headed for the river.

"Are we so tired and hungry for a true prophet after hundreds of years," Jason asked, "that we up and leave our houses and our fields and set out at the mere mention that a man might bring us some new wisdom, some special consolation?"

"Has it really been four hundred years," asked his uncle Jacimus, "since a prophet has spoken or are we simply deaf to the prophets whom the Lord sends? I can't help but wonder."

Inevitably men quarreled over the Temple. They quarreled over whether or not the Temple was too Greek, too huge, too filled with books and teachers and money changers, and crowds of gaping eager Gentiles, always being warned to stay out of the inner courts, always being threatened with death if they did not obey the laws, and as to the priesthood, Joseph Caiaphas and his father-in-law, Annas, well, men had plenty to say on that matter as well.

"One thing is clear as to Caiaphas," my uncle Cleopas interjected whenever he could. "The man's withstood the political currents a long time."

"You say that because he's your kinsman," came a rejoinder.

"No, I say it because it's true," said Cleopas, and quickly he rattled off the names of High Priests come and gone, including those once appointed by the House of Herod and later by the Romans.

This question of the Roman appointment of our High Priests could start a regular battle. But there were enough older men to quiet the hotheads, and even Hananel spoke up once or twice to put down with contempt any talk of purifying the Temple as the Essenes so longed to do. "That," he averred, "is idle talk. It is our Temple!"

All my life I'd heard this sort of argument, these musings. Sometimes I followed the thread. Most of the time my mind drifted. No one expected a word from me one way or the other.

Most of those falling in with us did not know that John bar Zechariah was our near cousin. Those who did were silenced fairly quickly by our simple admissions that we knew very little of him, that decades and miles had separated us completely.

I'd last seen John when I was a boy of seven.

Jason of course could rather vividly describe him, but it always came down to the same interesting yet remote picture: studious, pious, a model among the Essenes—who had then vanished for the even harsher life of the broiling desert.

My mother, who might have more stories of John and his parents than anyone present, said nothing. My mother, in the months before my birth, had gone to lodge with Elizabeth and Zechariah, and it was from those days that the stories came which Jason had repeated to me—my mother's song of happiness, the prophecy of Zechariah at his son's birth. These were all things well known to my mother.

But she had no care now, any more than she'd ever had, to join in the conversation of the Pharisees and the Scribes, and the young nephews, and occasional nieces, who knew only bits and pieces of these things, and were hungry for more.

Jason kept his secrets too, though I could see many a night by the fire, he was bursting with the desire to stand up and recite from memory every prayer he'd learnt from John which had come down from John's father and mother and my mother.

I gave him a little smile now and then, and he would wink and shake his head; but he accepted that these were not his tales to tell. And on went the arguments as to who was this John to whom we were all so devoutly committing ourselves.

As we left the high hills of Galilee and went down into the Jordan Valley, we came into the more welcome and warmer air. It was dry at first. Then we were as close to the reedy marshes along the river as we could come, and every hour brought fresh news that John, approaching from the south as he ministered, was even closer to us perhaps than we thought. And we might on any day come directly upon him.

Joseph was not well.

Joseph took to sleeping in the wagon, constantly, and it sent a shiver through James and through me to see it, the manner of this deep unbroken sleep. We all knew this kind of slumber. We all knew this strange rhythmical breathing, the seemingly effortless way it went on over the clatter of the wheels and the inevitable heave of rocks and ruts.

The women marked it, without question, but seemed more patient with it than was my uncle Cleopas or my younger brothers, who would waken Joseph at the slightest excuse.

"Let him rest," said my mother. Aunt Esther ordered them all to do the same.

The look in my mother's eye was sad as it had been the night we'd received the letter. But she was steady in her sadness. Nothing surprised her, or alarmed her. She sat beside Joseph from time to time, between him and her brother, Cleopas. She cradled Joseph against her shoulder. She gave him water when he did stir, but in general she kept the others from rousing him which they did principally to comfort themselves that he could indeed be roused.

One night Joseph woke and did not know where we were. No matter what we said, we couldn't make him understand it, that we were headed to the Jordan to meet with John bar Zechariah and his following there. James even took out the rumpled letter and read it over to him in the waning light.

Finally my mother said, "Do you think we would take you where you don't want to go? We would never do that. You sleep now."

He was immediately comforted, and closed his eyes.

James went off alone so that no one could see him cry. This was his father who was leaving us. Oh, we were all brothers, but this was the father of James by a young wife whom none of us, except Alphaeus and Cleopas, had ever known. As a little boy, James had been at his mother's deathbed along with Joseph. And soon now too Joseph would be gone.

I went to be near to James, and when he wanted, he beckoned for me to come. He was troubled as always, turning this way and that. "I shouldn't have insisted he come."

"But you didn't," I said, "and he wants to come, and tomorrow when the sun rises . . . we will be there."

"But what can it mean, this, that one baptizes another,

that one does not go down into the river to bathe on one's own as always, but that another . . . And look, will you, at the soldiers? Word of all this will rouse this fool of a Governor, you know it will."

I knew he needed to have all these cares so that he would not face the one care, that Joseph was dying. So I didn't say anything to him. And soon enough he went off to argue the matter again and again with Jason, Reuben, Hananel, the Rabbi, and the most recent group of the King's soldiers, several of whom accompanied the rich who traveled in brilliantly colored litters—and I stood looking back at the huge company, spilling over the rocky ground, and then up at the darkening sky.

The warm air was sweet with the scent of the river and the green marshes, and I could hear the cry of the birds who always gathered in the vicinity of the river. I liked it, and my heart was tripping, and I too felt that sadness again, as I'd felt it with my mother. It was light yet terrible. It made for a kind of drifting and amazement at the smallest and most trivial things.

Something was changing and forever. The children, summoned now to go to sleep whether they liked it or not, had no sense of this change, only of novelty and adventure, as they might on an excursion to the great sea.

Even my brothers had lapsed into a wary exultation which they defined decisively to one another as they agreed that they would confess, be washed, indeed allow themselves to be baptized if that is what John bar Zechariah insisted upon, and they would return to this or that chore, and this or that problem of life—with renewed strength.

In me there was a wholly different awareness. I did not press for speed, and I did not lag behind. I did not lament the distance one way or the other. I moved slowly towards what was at last going to separate me from all around me. I knew this. I knew it without knowing how or what would actually happen. And the only place I saw this same awareness—and some measure of this same acceptance—was in my mother's soft, habitual gaze.

20

It was midmorning, under a gray and blustering sky, when we came upon the entire baptismal gathering.

Even our own numbers had not prepared us for the size of it, the great spreading mass of people on both sides of the river, stretching out as far as we could see, and many with broad, richly decorated tents, and feasts laid out on their rugs, while others were the masses of the downtrodden who'd come to stand side by side with the Priests and Scribes, in their ragged garments.

Cripples, beggars, the very old, and even the painted women of the streets made up part of the crowd, along with all those who'd mixed with us in coming.

The King's soldiers were everywhere, and we recognized the apparel of those who served King Herod Antipas here, and those who served his brother, Philip, there, and all around were splendidly clad women, flanked by their servants, or just emerging from their sumptuous litters.

When we finally caught sight of John himself, the crowd was hushed, and the anthems being sung were a distant backdrop. Here men and women removed their outer robes, and went down only in their tunics into the water, and some men removed even these to proceed in their loincloths, as they approached the clear figure of John himself and his many disciples.

Everywhere around us were the secretive whispers of those confessing their sins, begging for forgiveness from the Lord, murmuring just loud enough for a voice to be heard but no real words, as eyes were closed and garments dropped in the reeds, and people wandered on into the marsh and then into the river.

The disciples of John were to the left and the right of him.

And he himself was unmistakable. Tall, with this shaggy black hair streaming over his shoulders and down his back, he received one pilgrim after another, his dark eyes shining brilliantly in the gray morning light, his voice low and carrying over the rumble of voices around him.

"Repent, for the Kingdom of Heaven is at hand," he declared, each time as though it were the first, and those around him took up the saying, until we soon perceived it was a very chanting, a chanting that mingled in timbre and pitch from time to time with the random and ceaseless confessions.

Jason and the young men stood back, arms folded, watching. But one by one my brothers went down, stripping off their robes, and entered into the water.

I saw James go down under the current and rise up slowly as John, his face unchanged by any conceivable recognition, poured a conch of water over his head.

Joses, Judas, and Simon moved towards the disciples, their sons and nephews moving with them. Menachim had taken Little Isaac by the hand and led him down close beside him as he seemed wary of the spongy earth and the dense reeds, and the river itself though the depth of it didn't rise above the knees of those who stood in it.

A high tent mounted on four ornate poles flapped in the wind loudly as the gray clouds glided over the radiant sun. Out of it came a rich toll collector, a man I knew in passing only from the inevitable journeys to work or visit in Capernaum.

He stood beside me, staring at the great shifting mass of the baptizers and the baptized, and indeed the core of the crowd seemed to swell and stretch out to the right and left as we watched it.

Out of the gathering behind us, thrusting himself between us, came a Pharisee, beautifully garbed and with a long white beard, and beside him two men who were obviously Priests in their finest linen garments.

"By whose authority do you do this!" demanded the white-bearded Pharisee. "Come now, John bar Zechariah. If you are not Elijah, then who are you that you draw men here for the forgiveness of sins? Who are your disciples?"

John stopped and looked up.

The sun behind the gray clouds made John squint as he tried to pick out the man who was challenging him. His eyes passed over me and the toll collector.

Again the Pharisee declared, "By whose authority do you dare to bring these people here."

"Bring them? I haven't brought them!" John answered. His voice rang out effortlessly over the entire throng. He drew in his breath as one used to speaking above noise or wind.

"I've told you. I am not Elijah. I am not the Christ. I have told you that He who comes after me is before me!" He appeared to gain strength as he spoke.

The disciples went on baptizing the pilgrims.

I saw Avigail, fully robed, descend into the river. I realized the young man who beckoned to her, who lifted his conch and directed her to kneel in the water, was in fact my young cousin John bar Zebedee. There he was, in his wet and clinging robes, his hair long and unkempt, a boy of twenty beside the man who cried out now for all to hear:

"I tell you again, you are a brood of vipers! And you will not be safe declaring yourselves the sons of Abraham. I tell you the Lord can raise up sons of Abraham from these very stones. Even as I stand here, the axe is being laid to the root of the tree. Every tree that does not bear good fruit will be cut down, and cast into the fire!"

All throughout the crowd people looked to the Rabbis and the Priests who were moving forward at the sound of John's voice.

Jason called out suddenly,

"But John, whence comes your authority to declare these things to us! This is what all men want to know."

John looked up, but did not appear to recognize Jason any more than he recognized any particular man, and he answered:

"Haven't I told you? I will tell you again. 'I'm the voice of one crying in the wilderness, "Make ready the way of the Lord, make His paths straight. Every ravine shall be filled, and every mountain and hill will be brought low; the crooked will become straight, and the rough roads smooth . . . and all flesh will see the salvation of God!" ' "

It seemed to the farthest reaches the crowd could hear him. People cried out in thanks, and more and more went down into the river. Jason and Reuben went down into the river.

I saw James come up the bank, his long loose hair still very wet, and he reached out for Joseph—and James and my mother took Joseph down together.

The toll collector watched as this aged man made his descent.

John received Joseph himself, though again I saw no recognition in John's eyes of this man and this woman who stood before him. They entered the water as everyone else was doing; and over their heads he poured the water from his conch.

Shouts greeted him again from the crowd.

This time it was Shemayah who burst out suddenly, as though he couldn't contain himself:

"Then what are we to do!"

"Need I tell you?" John answered. He drew back and once again raised his voice with the effortless power of an orator. "The man among you who has two tunics is to share with the man who has none; and those of you who have food are to give it to those who have nothing!"

Suddenly the young toll collector beside me called out, "Teacher, what shall *we* do!" People turned their heads to see who put this passionate question, so much from his own heart.

"Ah, collect no more than what you have been ordered to collect," John responded. A huge wave of approving murmurs moved through those on the banks. The toll collector nodded his head.

But the King's soldiers were now stepping forward. "And what do you say to us, Teacher!" one shouted. "Tell us, what can we do?"

John looked up at them, squinting once more against the silvery clouded sun. "Don't take money by force, that's what you can do. And never accuse anyone falsely, and be content with your wages."

Again came the nods and murmurs of approval.

"I tell you, the One coming after me already has His winnowing fork in His hand to clear His threshing floor, and to gather His wheat into the barn, or to burn up the chaff with unquenchable fire."

Many went down who'd not done so before, but a huge commotion shook the crowd suddenly. People were turning, and there were cries of amazement.

Far to the right and above me on the slope there appeared a large group of soldiers, and out of their midst there strode one quite recognizable figure, stunning everyone to silence as he approached the bank over the river. The soldiers beat back the very grass for him, and held up the edges of his long purple cloak.

It was Herod Antipas. Seldom had I ever seen him so close to me as he stood now—a tall man, impressive by anyone's standards, and gentle eyed as he looked down in wonder on the man baptizing in the middle of the river.

"John bar Zechariah," the King cried. An uneven and rapid hush fell over all those who saw him, all who heard his voice.

John looked up. Again he squinted. Then he raised his hand to shade his eyes.

"What is it that I must do?" the King cried out. "Tell me. How must I repent?"

The King's face was narrow and grave, but there was no mockery in him, only an intense focus.

John didn't speak for a moment and then in a huge voice he replied.

"Give up your brother's wife. She is not your wife. You know the law! Are you not a Jew?"

The crowd was shocked. The soldiers drew in close to the King as if anticipating a command, but the King himself was very still, and only watched as John reached out now to take the shoulders of my beloved Joseph, and help him up out of the water.

The toll collector started towards my mother and James,

in order to give them assistance. Then he tossed off his rich mantle, and let it fall like any common wool robe, and he stepped before John and went down on his knees as all the others had done before him.

Joseph watched as the toll collector dipped his head and came up, wiping the water away from his face. The droplets clung to his oiled and gleaming hair.

The King stood impassive on the bluff, and then without a word, he turned, and disappeared into the ranks of his soldiers, and the entire flock, with sparkling gold-tipped lances and rounded shields, moved out of sight and was swallowed by the pilgrims coming towards us.

Dozens of men and women headed towards the water.

I saw Joseph staring up at me, his eyes clear, his expression familiar.

I moved down into the river. I passed Joseph and my mother, and the toll collector who stood at Joseph's elbow ready to assist him, on account of his age, even as James was there.

I moved up in front of John bar Zechariah.

My way had always been to look down. The subject of whisper and insult through much of my life, I seldom confronted a man with my gaze, but rather turned away and sought my work as a matter of course. It was a quiet demeanor.

But I didn't do this now. It was no longer my way. That was gone.

He stood frozen, staring at me. I looked at him—at his rugged frame, the hair matted to his chest, the dark camel-skin cloak half covering him. I saw his eyes then fixed on mine.

They were glazed, his eyes, the inevitable defense against a multitude of faces, a multitude of gazes, a multitude of expectations.

But as we faced one another—he only slightly taller than I—his eyes softened. They lost their tight puckering, their deep distance. I heard the breath pass out of him.

There came a sound like the flapping of wings, gentle yet large, as of doves startled in the dovecote, and all struggling Heavenward.

He stared upwards, to the right and left, then back at me. He hadn't found the source of the sound.

I addressed him now in Hebrew:

"Johanan bar Zechariah," I said.

His eyes grew wide.

"Yeshua bar Joseph," he said.

The toll collector drew in to watch, to hear. I could see the vague shape of my mother and Joseph nearby. I could feel the others turning slowly towards us, moving clumsily towards us.

"It's you!" John whispered. "You . . . baptize me!" He held up the conch, dripping with water.

The disciples to the right and left stopped in the very midst of what they did. Those coming up out of the water remained standing, attentive. Something had changed in the holy man. What had changed?

I felt the throng itself like a great connected and living thing breathing with us.

I held up my hands.

"We're made in His image, you and I," I said. "This is flesh, is it not? Am I not a man? Baptize me as you've done everyone else; do this, in the name of righteousness."

I went down into the water. I felt his hand on my left shoulder. I felt his fingers close on my neck. I saw nothing and felt nothing and heard nothing but the cool flooding water, and then slowly I came up out of it, and stood, shocked by the flood of sunlight.

The clouds above had shifted. The sound of beating wings filled my ears. I stared forward and saw across John's face the shadow of a dove moving upwards—and then I saw the bird itself rising into a great opening of deep blue sky, and I heard a whisper against my ears, a whisper that penetrated the sound of the wings, as though a pair of lips had touched both ears at the same time, and faint as it was, soft and secretive as it was, it seemed the edge of an immense echo.

This is my Son, this is my beloved.

All the riverbank had gone quiet.

Then noise. The old familiar noise. Shouts and cries, and exclamations, those sounds so mingled in my mind and soul with the stoning of Yitra and the mob around Avigail—the noise of triumphant young men, the endless broken crying of pilgrims—I heard them all around me, the excited beat and cry of voices intermingling with one another, answering one another, growing louder and louder as they vied with one another.

I stared upward at the great endless stretch of blue and I saw the dove flying higher and higher. It became a tiny thing, a speck in the shimmer of the drenching sunlight.

I staggered backwards. I almost lost my balance. I stared at Joseph. I saw his gray eyes fixed on me, saw the faint smile on his lips, and saw in the same instant my mother's face, impassive and still faintly sad, lovingly sad, as she stood beside him.

"It is You!" said John bar Zechariah again.

I didn't answer.

The chorus of the crowd rose.

I turned and went up the far bank, tramping through the weeds, moving faster and faster. I stopped and glanced back once. I saw Joseph again, held tenderly in the arms of the toll collector who stared at me wildly. Joseph's face was collected and wistful and over the gulf between us he nodded. I saw my brothers, I saw all of my kindred there, I saw Shemayah, I saw Avigail. I saw the small figure of Silent Hannah.

I saw them all, and I saw them particularly—the smooth innocence of the very old, eyes gleaming beneath the heavy folds of skin; the sudden break from weariness in those in their prime, who stood poised between condemnation and wonder; the frank excitement of the children who begged for their parents to explain to them what had happened—and interwoven with all, the busy, the concerned, the worn, the confused, each and every one touching another.

Never had I beheld them all in this way, each anchored to concern yet wedded to the one to the left and the one to the right, and all tossing as if not in sand but by the sea on rolling waves.

I turned and looked down at John, who'd turned to stare up at me. He opened his mouth to speak but said nothing.

I turned away from him. For one second the sunshine sparkling in the stiff branches of a shifting tree held me frozen. If trees and blowing grass could talk, they were talking to me.

And they were talking of silence.

On and on I walked, my mind filled only with the sound of my own feet, moving through reeds and marsh and then to the rocky dry ground, and on and on, my sandals slapping the road, and then the bare earth where there was no road.

I had now to be alone, to go where no one could find me or question me. Not now. I had to seek the solitude that all my life had been denied me.

I had to seek it beyond hamlet or town or camp. I had to seek it where there was nothing but the burnt sand, and the searing wind, and the highest cliffs of the land. I had to seek it as if it was nowhere and as if it contained nothing—when in fact it was the palm of the hand that held me.

21

VOICES. THEY WOULDN'T STOP.

I'd passed the last little settlement days ago. I'd drunk my last deep draught of water there.

I didn't know where I was now, only that it was cold, and the only true sound was the wind howling as it swept down into the wadi. I clung to the cliff and made my way upwards. The light was dying fast. That's why it was so cold.

And the voices wouldn't stop, all the arguments, all the calculations, all the predications, all the pondering, and on and on, and on.

The wearier I became the louder they became.

In a small cave I lay, out of the bite of the wind, and drew my robe tightly around me. The thirst was gone. The hunger was gone. So that meant it had been many days because they'd hurt for many days and that much was now finished. Light-headed, empty, I craved all things and no one thing. My lips split and the skin flaked from them. My hands were burnt red; my eyes ached whether opened or closed.

But the voices would not stop, and slowly, rolling over on my back, I looked beyond the entrance of the cave at the stars—just as I'd always done, musing at the sheer cloudless clarity of it over the sandy wastes, the thing we call magnificence.

And then the remembering came, driving away the random voices of censure, the remembering . . . of every single solitary thing I'd ever done in this, my earthly existence.

It was not a sequence. It did not have the order of words written on parchment from one side of the column to the other, and then back again and again and again. Yet it was unfolding.

And sparkling in the density were the moments of pain—of loss, of fear, of sudden regret, of grief, of discomforting and tormented amazement.

Pain, like the stars themselves, each moment with its own infinitesimal shape and magnitude. All of those memories drew themselves around me as if composing a great garment that was my life, a garment that wrapped itself around and around and over and under until it encased me like my skin, completely.

Sometime before morning, I understood something. That I could without the slightest effort hold any and all of these moments in my mind; that they coexisted, these varied and tiny and countless agonies. Little agonies.

When the morning came and the bitter wind died in the glare, I walked on, letting these countless moments come, letting my mind fling them in my own eyes and at my own heart, like the sand that burnt my eyes, and burnt my lips. I went on remembering.

In the night I awoke. Was this my own voice reciting what was written? " 'And every secret thing shall be opened, and every dark place illuminated.' "

Dear God, no, do not let them know this, do not let them know the great accumulation of all of this, this agony and joy, this misery, this solace, this reaching, this gouging pain, this . . .

But they will know, each and every one of them will know. They will know because what you are remembering is what has happened to each and every one of them. Did you think this was more or less for you? Did you think—?

And when they are called to account, when they stand naked before God and every incident and utterance is laid bare—you, you will know all of it with each and every one of them!

I knelt in the sand.

Is this possible, Lord, to be with each of them when he or she comes to know? To be there for every single cry of anguish? For the grief-stricken remembrance of every incomplete joy?

Oh, Lord, God, what is judgment and how can it be, if I cannot bear to be with all of them for every ugly word, every harsh and desperate cry, for every gesture examined, for every deed explored to its roots? And I saw the deeds, the deeds of my own life, the smallest, most trivial things, I saw them suddenly in their seed and sprout and with their groping branches; I saw them growing, intertwining with other deeds, and those deeds come to form a thicket and a woodland and a great roving wilderness that dwarfed the world as we hold it on a map, the world as we hold it in our minds. Dear God, next to this, this endless spawning of deed from deed and word from word and thought from thought—the world is nothing. Every single soul is a world!

I started to cry. But I would not close off this vision—no, let me see, and all those who lifted the stones, and I, I blundering, and James' face when I said it, *I am weary of you, my brother,* and from that instant outwards a million echoes of those words in all present who heard or thought they heard, who would remember, repeat, confess, defend . . . and so on it goes for the lifting of a finger, the launching of the ship, the fall of an army in a northern forest, the burning of a city as flames rage through house after house! Dear God, I cannot . . . but I will. *I will.*

I sobbed aloud. I will. O Father in Heaven, I am reaching to You with hands of flesh and blood. I am longing for You in Your perfection with this heart that is imperfection! And I reach up for You with what is decaying before my very eyes, and I stare at Your stars from within the prison of this body, but this is not my prison, this is my Will. *This is Your Will.*

I collapsed weeping.

And I will go down, down with every single one of them into the depths of Sheol, into the private darkness, into the anguish exposed for all eyes and for Your eyes, into the fear, *into the fire which is the heat of every mind.* I will be with them, every solitary one of them. *I am one of them! And I am Your Son! I am Your only begotten Son! And driven here by Your Spirit, I cry because I cannot do anything but grasp it, grasp it as I cannot contain it in this flesh-and-blood mind, and by Your leave I cry.*

I cried. I cried and I cried. "*Lord, give me this little while that I may cry, for I've heard that tears accomplish much. . . .*"

Alone? You said you wanted to be alone? You wanted this, to be alone? You wanted the silence? You wanted to be alone and in the silence. Don't you understand the temptation now of being alone? You *are* alone. Well, you are absolutely alone because you *are the only One who can do this!*

What judgment can there ever be for man, woman, or child—if I am not there for every heartbeat at every depth of their torment?

The dawn came.

And the dawn came again, and again.

I lay in a heap as the sand blew over me.

And the voice of the Lord was not in the wind; and it was

not in the sand; and it was not in the sun; and it was not in the stars.

It was inside me.

I'd always known who I really was. I was God. And I'd chosen not to know it. Well, now I knew just what it meant to be the man who knew he was God.

22

FORTY DAYS AND FORTY NIGHTS. That's how long
Moses remained on Sinai. That's how long Elijah fasted
before the Lord spoke to him.

"Lord, I have done it," I whispered. "I know, too, what
they expect of me. Only too well, do I know."

My sandals were falling to pieces. I'd retied the thongs
more times than I could count. The sight of my sunburnt
hands unsettled me, but I only laughed under my breath. I
was headed home.

Down the mountains, towards the bright shimmering
desert that lay between me and the river I couldn't see.

"Alone, alone, alone," I sang. I had never felt such hunger.
I had never felt such thirst. They rose as if in answer to my
own pronouncement. "Oh, yes, so many times did I devoutly
wish for it," I sang to myself. "To be alone." And now I was
alone, with no bread, no water, no place to rest my head.

"Alone?"

It was a voice. It was a familiar voice, a man's voice familiar in timbre and pitch.

I turned around.

The sun was behind me, and so the light was painless and
clear.

He was about my height, and beautifully garbed, more beautifully and richly even than Reuben of Cana or Jason—more like the figure of the King. He wore a linen tunic, embroidered with a border of green leaves and red flowers, each little floret glistening with gold thread. The border of his white mantle was even thicker, richer, woven as the mantles of the Priests are woven, and hung even with tiny gold bells. His sandals were covered with gleaming buckles. And around his waist he wore a thick leather girdle studded with bronze points, as a soldier might wear. Indeed a sword in a jeweled scabbard hung at his side.

His hair was long and lustrous, a deep rich brown. And so were his soft eyes.

"My little joke does not amuse you," he said gently with a graceful bow.

"Your joke?"

"You don't ever look into a mirror. Don't you recognize the image of yourself?"

A shock spread over my face, and then all of my skin. He was my duplicate, except I'd never seen myself in such attire.

He made a small circle in the sand so that I might better see the picture he made. I was fascinated at the expression—or lack of it—in his large puckering eyes.

"You might say," he began, "that I feel some obligation to remind you of what you are? You see, I'm aware of your particular delusion. You don't hold yourself to be a mere prophet or a holy man, like your cousin John. You think you're the Lord Himself."

I didn't reply.

"Oh, I know. You wanted to keep it a secret, and you do indeed often veil your mind quite well, or so it seems to me, but out here in this wilderness? Well, too often, you've murmured aloud."

He drew closer, lifting the edge of his sleeve so that he

himself might admire the embroidery, the sharply pointed leaves, the flowers exploding in crimson thread.

"Of course you're not going to talk to me, are you?" he said with a faint sneer. I looked like that when I sneered. If I ever had.

"But I know you're hungry, dreadfully hungry. So hungry you'd do almost anything to have something to eat. You're devouring your own flesh and blood."

I turned and started to walk away.

"Now, if you are a holy man of God," he said, catching up with me, and walking alongside me, staring at me eye to eye when I glanced at him, "and we'll forget the delusion for the moment that you're the Creator of the Universe, then you can surely turn these stones, any of them here, into warm bread."

I stopped. I was overcome with the scent of it, warm bread. I could feel it in my mouth.

"This would be no problem for Elijah," he said, "or for Moses for that matter. And you do claim to be a holy one of God, don't you? Son of God? Beloved Son? Do it. Make the stones bread."

I stared down at the stones, and then I started walking again.

"Very well then," he said, keeping pace with me, the bells jingling softly as he walked. "Let's return to your delusion. You are God. Now according to your cousin, God can raise up sons of Abraham from these stones, or those stones, or any stones, no? Well, then make these stones into bread. You need it badly enough, don't you?"

I turned and laughed at him. " 'Man doesn't live by bread alone,' " I answered him, " 'but by everything that proceeds from the mouth of God.' "

"What a wretchedly literal translation," he said, shaking

his head, "and may I point out to you, my pious and deluded one, that your clothes have hardly been preserved during these mere forty days, like those of your ancestors in the forty years they wandered, but that you are a ragged beggar who will very soon be barefoot as well?"

I laughed again. "Nevertheless," I said, "I'm going on my way."

"Well," he said before I started, "it's too late for you to bury your father. That's been done."

I stopped.

"Oh, what, don't tell me the prophet whose birth was accompanied with so many signs and wonders doesn't know that his father, Joseph, is dead?"

I didn't answer. I felt my heart grow big and begin to throb in my ears. I looked out over the sandy wastes.

"Since you seem at best to be a sometime prophet," he went on in the same calm voice, my voice, "let me give you the picture. It was in a toll collector's tent that he breathed his last, and in a toll collector's arms, can you imagine, though his son sat nearby and your mother wept. And do you know how he spent his last few hours? Recounting to the toll collector and anyone else who happened to hear all he could remember of your birth—oh, you know the old song about the angel coming to your poor terrified mother, and the long trek to Bethlehem so that you might come howling into the world in the midst of the worst weather, and then the visit of angels on high to shepherds, of all people, and those men. The Magi. He told the toll collector about their coming as well. And then he died, raving, you might say, only softly so."

I looked forward, down at the desert floor. How far was it to the river?

"Weeping! Well, look, you are weeping," he said. "I never expected it. I expected you to be properly ashamed that such a righteous man would die in the arms of a well-respected thief, but I didn't expect such tears. After all, you did walk off and leave the old man at the river, did you not?"

I didn't answer.

He whistled to himself, idly, a little song such as one might whistle or hum as one strolled, and stroll he did around me in a circle as I stood there.

"Well," he said, squaring off in front of me. "You are tenderhearted, we know that much. But a prophet? I think not. As for the delusion that you created the entire world, well, let me remind you of what you no doubt already know: a delusion similar to that cost me my place above in the Heavenly Court."

"I think you gloss it over," I said. My voice was thick with tears, but my tears were drying in the hot desert wind.

"Ah, you speak to me, not to quote Scripture, but in actual words," he said. He laughed in a perfect imitation of my earlier laugh, and flashed a warm smile at me that was almost pretty.

"You know, holy men almost never do speak to me at all. They write long sonorous poetry about my speaking to the Lord of Creation and His speaking to me, but they themselves, the scribes? At the mere mention of my name, they run shrieking in dread."

"And you do so love to have your name mentioned, don't you?" I said. "No matter what name it is." I went on slowly. "Ahriman, Mastema, Satanel, Satan, Lucifer . . . you love it, don't you, when you're addressed?"

He was silenced.

"Beelzebub," I said. "Is that your favorite?" I said it in Greek: "Lord of the Flies."

"I loathe that name!" he said with a flare of rage. "I will not answer to any of those names," he said.

"Of course you won't. What name could ever rescue you from the chaos that's your very purpose?" I asked. "Demon, devil, adversary." I shook my head. "No, don't answer to them. Don't answer to the name Azazel, either. Names are what you dream of, names and purpose and hope, of which you have none."

I turned and started to walk on.

He caught up with me.

"Why are you talking to me?" he asked in a perfect rage.

"Why are *you* talking to *me!*"

"Signs and wonders," he said, the blood flaring in his cheeks—or so he would have it seem. "Too many signs and wonders surround you, my miserable ragged friend. And I've talked to you before. I came to you once in your dreams."

"I remember," I said. "And you took on the raiment of beauty then too. It must be something you want so badly."

"You know nothing of me. You have no idea! I was the firstborn of the Lord you claim as your father, you miserable beggar."

"Careful," I said. "If you become too angry you may dissolve in a puff of smoke."

"This is no jest, you fledgling prophet," he said. "I don't come and go at whim."

"Go at whim," I said. "That will be sufficient."

"Do you know who I really am?" he asked, and his face was broken suddenly with grief. "Well, I will tell you." And in Hebrew, he spoke the words: "Helel ben-Shahar."

"Bright sun of morning," I said. I raised my right hand and snapped my fingers. "I see you falling . . . like that."

A terrific roar went up around me, and the sand went flying as if a storm had come out of the placid sunlight and was about to carry me down the cliff.

I felt myself drawn upwards with spectacular speed and

suddenly another roar, more familiar and immense, surrounded me, and I stopped short at the edge of the parapet of the Temple, the Temple in Jerusalem, under the huge sky, and above the enormous crowds of those who wandered in and out of it. I was standing on the pinnacle. I was looking down into the vast lower courts.

The sounds and scents of the crowd rose up in my nostrils. I felt the hunger so deeply it was a pain. And out on all sides lay the rooftops of Jerusalem while the people swarmed below in its tangle of narrow streets.

"Look on all this," he said beside me.

"And why should I?" I asked. "It's not really there."

"No? You don't believe it? You think it's an illusion?"

"You're full of illusions and lies."

"Then fling yourself down, now, from this height. Fling yourself down into that crowd. We'll see if it's an illusion. And what if it is not? Is it not written, 'He will give His angels charge of you, and on their hands they will bear you up, lest you strike your foot against a stone.' "

"Oh, you have been a murderer from the beginning," I said. "You would so love to see me tumble, downwards, see my bones break, see this face you so clearly imitate bruised and shattered, but it's more than that you want, isn't it? The body's nothing to you, no matter how mercilessly you torment it. You want my soul."

"No, you are wrong," he said in a low voice, leaning as close to me as he could. "And we are here, yes, I've brought you here, not by illusions and lies, but to show you the very place where you must begin your work. It's you who claim to be the Christ. It's you whom others herald as the Son of David, the prince who will lead his people to victory in battle, it's you and your people who have celebrated your great power and eventual conquest in book after book, and poem after poem. Throw yourself down! I say, Do it, and let the angels sweep you up. Let your battle begin with that pact between you and the Lord you claim to serve!"

"I will not put the Lord to the test here," I said. "And that too is written, 'You shall not tempt the Lord your God.' "

"Where then will you begin your battle?" he asked as if he sincerely wanted to know. "How will you raise your armies? How will you proclaim your message throughout the Jews of all this land and the next and the next after that? How will you get word to the far-flung communities of Jews throughout the Empire that it's time for them to buckle on sword and shield under your banner and in the name of your God?"

"I knew it when I was a child," I said, regarding him.

"Knew what?"

"You're the Lord of the Flies, but you're at the mercy of Time. You don't know what's to happen in time."

"Well, if that's true, than half the time, you're no better than I because you don't know it, and they are nothing, those vermin down there, those you call your brothers and sisters, because they know nothing moment to moment. At least you have visions, and schemes."

He reached out for me as if he'd take hold of me, and his face was twisted with malevolence.

"What have you known of time these dreary years you've spent in Nazareth? What is time in which you grind your aching muscles to dust, all of you? Why do you bear it? Why does He bear it? You claim to know His Will. Tell me, why doesn't He shut it down?"

"Shut down Time?" I asked in a small voice. "The gift of Time?"

"The gift? It's a gift to be lost in this miserable world of His, lost to the pitiless ignorance of others, in Time?"

"Ah, you do know one thing and that is misery," I said.

"I? I know misery? What misery do they know, day in and day out, and what misery have you known with them? Do you think this life and time was a gift to that boy Yitra, whom your villagers stoned? You know he was innocent, don't you? Oh, he was tempted, but he was innocent. And the Orphan? That child didn't even know why he died. Do you know what was in their hearts when they saw the stones coming at them? What do you think is in the heart of Yitra's mother, where she weeps, at this very *time*?"

"I would ask you where hope comes from, if not out of time? I would ask you that and give you that answer, but you've made your decision, whole and complete and forever, and for you there is no time."

"I should throw you down from here!" he whispered. He held up his hands to clutch at me, but they didn't close on my throat. "I should smash you on those stones. I have no qualms about tempting the Lord your God. I never have."

He stepped back, too furious for a moment to speak. Then he took a breath.

"Maybe you are some phantasm, made up out of His impassable and merciless Mind. How else could you not feel for Avigail when she stood terrified among those children, awaiting the very same death the village had given Yitra and the Orphan? Do you have mercy on any of them anywhere ever?"

The light changed. Then the air began to move.

The entire vision of the Temple and its daily multitude shifted, crumpled, as if it were pictures painted on silk.

I was in the whirlwind, and I reached out.

Suddenly we were standing together, the beautifully garbed one and me, on the crest of a mountain, perhaps the highest mountain in the land. Only it was in no certain land.

Beneath us stretched what appeared to be a map but was no map—rather the patterns of mountains and rivers and valleys and oceans that made up the entire world.

"That's right," he said over the faint wind. "The world. You see it as I see it. Beautiful to behold."

He stood for a moment as though earnestly contemplating this majestic perspective, and indeed I did look out on what he claimed to reveal, and then I looked at him.

He was in profile, my profile, his dark hair blown back away from his cheekbones, and his eyes were softened as mine often were, and he held his mantle rather gracefully and easily at his sides.

"Do you really want to help them?" he asked me. He lifted his finger. "I say truly—do you want to help them? Truly? Or do you really mean to frighten them and leave them far for the worse that another prophet has come cursing and denouncing and proclaiming what will never come to pass?"

He turned to me and his eyes filled with tears. No doubt too very like the tears he'd seen me shed only a while before. He pressed his hands together before his face and then he looked up at me through this dramatic and glittering mist.

"You have indeed come amid signs and wonders," he said thoughtfully, as though the words were pulled out of a soul. "And these are remarkable times. There are Jews in every city of the Empire. The Scripture of your God is in Greek for them to read no matter where they live or what their schooling. The name of your nameless God is spoken perhaps in the farthest reaches of the north. Who knows? And you, a filthy carpenter, yes, but you are the Son of David and you are very clever and you do speak well."

"Thank you," I said.

"The Scriptures speak of one who'll lead them to independence and to triumph. And you know these Scriptures.

You knew what it meant when you were a child—the words—Christ the Lord."

"I did," I said.

"You can help them. You can lead the armies. You can draw on all those far-flung cells of the devout waiting to come to your support. Why, there are Jews in Rome who would bring you and your army into the city; with you at the lead, they'd storm the Emperor's Palace, they'd put an end to every last man in the Senate, and the Praetorian Guard. Can you see this? Can you imagine what I'm trying to explain to you?"

"I do see it," I said. "But it won't happen."

"But don't you understand, I'm trying to make plain to you that it can! You can gather them all from the cities to which they've wandered; you can bring these out of the Holy Land like a great whirlwind that can sweep the coasts of the entire sea."

"I follow you. I have from the start. It won't happen."

"But why won't it happen? Will you disappoint them? Will you utter prayers and make speeches like your cousin in the water of the river up to his knees performing empty gestures, and let them fall back into hating you because you've broken their hearts?"

I didn't answer.

"I'm offering you a victory your people haven't had for four hundred years," he said softly. "And if you do not do this thing, your people are finished. The world is swallowing them, Yeshua bar Joseph, the way that old man in Cana, that fool Hananel, said the world was swallowing you."

I didn't answer.

"It was finished for your people long ago," he went on intently, as if truly lost in his own thoughts. "It was finished when Alexander marched through this land and brought the Greek language with him and the Greek ways. It was smashed when the Romans overran this land, and they went into your very Temple, proving with a brutal fist that there was nothing, absolutely nothing, inside! If you don't give them this last chance, to come together around a mighty leader, your people will not die of hunger or thirst or by the sword or by the spear. They'll simply fade away. They're doing it already and they will go on doing it, forgetting their sacred language, mingling through wives and ambitious youths with Romans and Greeks and Egyptians until no one any longer remembers the Tongue of the Angels, until no one even remembers the name Jew. I give it what? A hundred years? Without a victory, it won't take that long. It will be finished. It will be as if it never was."

"Ah, cursed and designing Spirit," I said. "Do you remember nothing of Heaven? Surely you know that there are things unfolding in the womb of Time that are beyond your dreams, and sometimes beyond mine."

"What, what is unfolding?" he said. "The world gets bigger with every passing year and you become smaller, you people of the One True God, you people of the Nameless God who would have no gods before Him. You haven't converted them to your ways, and they eat you alive. I'm holding out to you the one thing that can save them, don't you see? And once this map the Romans have drawn for you is under your control, then you can teach them all the Laws He gave you on the Holy Mountain. I'm willing to put this into your hands!"

"You? You want to help me? And help us? Why?"

"Pay heed to me, fool. I'm running out of patience. Nothing is done here without me. Nothing. Not the simplest victory is accomplished unless I'm part of it. And this is my world, and these are all my nations. Will you not get down on your knees and worship me?"

His face crumpled. His tears flowed.

Was this how I looked when I was sad? When I wept?

He shivered as if this wind of his own creating was making him cold. And he stared out over the whole world of his own envisioning with a desperate, sorrowful gaze.

For a moment I forgot him.

I forgot completely that he was there. I looked out, and I saw something, something I'd glimpsed before, in the study of Hananel in Cana, and something I saw vividly now. Altars falling, thousands upon thousands of altars tumbling down as if the quaking of the earth itself were dislodging them, and on top of them fell their idols, marble and bronze and gold shattering, the dust rising as the fragments scattered. And it seemed the sound rolled on and on over the world he'd laid out before me, over the map he'd quickened for my benefit, but as I saw it, it was the world. All the altars going down.

Christ the Lord.

"What is it?" he demanded. "What did you say?"

I turned and looked at him, awakening from this terrible vision, this great sweep of destruction. I saw him again, vividly, in his finery, his skin no less fine than his costly robes.

"Those aren't your nations," I said. "The kingdoms of this world aren't yours. They never were."

"Of course they're mine," he said. It was almost a hiss. "I am the ruler of this world and I always have been. I am its Prince."

"No," I said. "None of it belongs to you. It never has."

"Worship me," he said gently, beguilingly, "and I will show you what is mine. I will give you the victory of which your prophets sang."

"The Lord on High is the One whom I worship, and no one else," I said. "You know this, you know it with every lie you speak. And you, you rule nothing and you never have." I pointed. "Look down, yourself, on this perspective that is so dear to you. Think of the thousands upon thousands who rise each day and go to sleep without ever thinking evil or doing evil, whose hearts are set upon their wives, their husbands, their fathers and mothers, their children, upon the harvest and the spring rain and the new wine and the new moon. Think of them in every land and every language, think of them as they hunger for the Word of God even where there is no one to give it to them, how they reach out for it, and how they turn from pain and misery and injustice, no matter what you would have them do!"

"Liar!" he said. He spit the word at me.

"Look at them, use your powerful eyes to see them everywhere around you," I said. "Use your powerful ears to hear their cheerful laughter, their natural songs. Look far and wide to find them coming together to celebrate the simple feasts of life from the deepest jungle to the great snowbound heights. What makes you think you rule these people! What, that one may falter, and another stumble, and someone in confusion fail to love as he has striven to do, or that some evil minion of yours can convulse the masses for a month of riot and ruin? Prince of this world!

"I'd laugh at you if you weren't unspeakable. You're the Prince of the Lie. And this is the lie: that you and the Lord God are equal, locked in combat with one another. That has *never* been so!"

He was near petrified with fury.

"You stupid, miserable little village prophet!" he said. "They'll laugh you out of Nazareth."

"It is the Lord God who rules," I said, "and He always has. You are nothing, and you have nothing and rule nothing. Not even your minions share with you in your emptiness and in your rage."

He was red faced, and speechless.

"Oh, yes, you have them, your minions. I've seen them. And you have your followers, those poor cursed souls you squeeze in your anxious fist. You even have your shrines. But how paltry are your grudging triumphs in this vast, vital world of blowing wheat and shining sun! How tawdry your attempts to rush into the breach of every petty dissension, to raise your puny standard over every hideous squabble or tenuous web of avarice and deceit—pathetic your one true possession: your lies! Your abominable lies! And always, always you seek to drive men to despair, to convince them in your envy and greed that your archenemy, the Lord God, is their enemy, that He is beyond their reach, beyond their pain, beyond their need. You lie! You have always lied! If you ruled this world you wouldn't offer to share a particle of it. You couldn't. There would be no world for you to share, because you would destroy it. You are yourself *The Lie!* And you are nothing other than that."

"Stop it, I demand that you stop!" he shouted. He put his hands up over his ears.

"It's I who've come to stop you!" I responded. "It's I who've come to reveal that your despair is a fraud! I'm here to tell one and all that you are no Ruler, and never were, that in the great scheme of things you are no more than a filthy brigand, a thief on the margins, a scavenger circling in impotent envy the camps of men and women! And I will destroy your Fabled Rule, as I destroy you—as I drive you out, stamp you out, blot you out—and not with hulking armies in baths of blood, not with the raging smoke and terror you so crave, not with swords and spears dripping with broken flesh. I will do it as you cannot imagine it—I will do it by family, by camp, by hamlet and village and town. I will do it at the banquet tables in the smallest rooms and greatest mansions of cities. I will do it heart by heart. I will do it soul by soul. Yes, the world is ready. Yes, the map is drawn. Yes, the Scripture goes forth in the common language of the world. Yes. And so I go on my way to do it, and you have struggled here once more—and forever—in vain."

I turned and moved forward, my feet finding the sure ground as I left him, and in a great sweeping wind, I was blinded for an instant, only to see the familiar slope emerge, the slope on which I'd walked when he first approached me, and below, for the first time, I saw in the far distance the misty streaks of green that marked the river's progress.

"You'll curse the day you refused me!" he shouted behind me.

I was sick. The hunger ate my insides. I was dizzy.

I looked back at him. He was still holding the illusion, his lovely garments gathered in graceful folds as he pointed to me.

"You take a good look at these soft clothes!" he shouted, mouth quivering like that of a child. "You'll never see yourself dressed in this manner again." He groaned. He doubled in pain as he groaned. He shook his fist at me.

I laughed and walked on.

He came up suddenly to my shoulder.

"You'll die on a Roman cross if you try to do this without me!" he said.

I stopped and faced him.

He stepped back, and then he fell back a great distance as if pushed by an invisible force. He scrambled for his balance.

"Get behind me, Satan," I said. "Get behind me!"

And in a great gust of wind, and rising sand, I heard him cry out and then the cry became a howling scream.

Now came the sandstorm in earnest. His howls were part of it, part of the relentless wind.

I felt myself fall, truly, and the cliff rose up in front of me, as the sand scraped my legs, my hands, and my face.

I twisted, and tumbled downwards, faster and faster, rolling with it, my arms drawn around my head. Down and down I fell.

My ears were filled with the wind, filled with his distant howls, and then softly there came that sound I'd heard at the river, that soft rush of wings.

I heard the flapping, the fluttering, the muffled beating of wings. All over me came the soft touch as if of hands, countless gentle hands, the even softer brush of lips—lips against my cheeks, my forehead, my parched eyelids. It seemed I was lost in a lovely weightless drift of song that had replaced the wind without true sound. And it carried me gently downwards; it embraced me; it ministered to me.

"No," I said. "No."

It became weeping now, this singing. It was pure and sad, yet irresistibly sweet. It had the immensity of joy. And there came more urgently these tender fingers, brushing my face and my burnt arms.

"No," I said. "I will do this. Leave me now. I will do it, as I've said."

I slipped away from them, or they spread out as soundlessly as they'd come, and rose and moved away in all directions, releasing me.

Alone again.

I was on the floor of the valley.

I was walking. My left sandal came loose. I stared down at it. I almost fell. I stooped to pick up what was left of it, this scrap of leather. On and on I walked, into the heated breeze.

23

THIS WAY AND THAT I listed and wandered, leaning on the wind, then righting myself, forcing myself to go forward.

Shapes appeared on the wavering horizon.

What seemed a small ship drifted there, and about it beings as if they floated in the heat as if it were the sea.

But this was not a ship and these were men on horseback.

Through the softly driving wind, I heard the horse approaching me. I saw it coming clearer and clearer.

I walked towards it. I heard a dim and terrible sound far off, beyond the horse, in the haze of green palms that marked the distant place that promised water.

The rider bore down on me.

"Holy Man," he cried out. He tried to control his horse. It danced past me, and he came back. He held out the skin of water.

"Holy Man, drink," he said. "Here."

I reached for it, and the skin moved up and down and away, like something bobbing on a string. I kept walking.

He jumped down from his horse, this man. Rich robes. Flash of rings.

"Holy Man," he said. He took my shoulder with one hand,

and with the other he brought the skin to my lips. He squeezed the skin. The water poured into my mouth. It spilled cold and delicious onto my tongue; it filled my mouth. It spilled down over my cracked lips and onto my burning chest.

I tried to take it in both hands. He steadied me.

"Not too much, my friend," he said. "Not too much, for you're starving."

He lifted the skin; he poured the water down over my head and I stood with eyes closed, feeling it wash my eyes, and my cheeks, feeling it slip into the itching heat inside my torn garments.

There came a howl—his howl!

I stopped and stared forward. The droplets were clinging to my lashes. That was no ship I had seen, but only the magnificent trappings of a rich tent in the distance.

The howl came again. *You dare!*

"My friend, forgive it," said the man beside me. "The sound you hear, it's my sister. Forgive her, Holy Man. We take her now to the Temple, one last time, to see if they can help her."

The howl rose again and broke into a huge and hoarse laughter.

A whisper touched my ear. *You'll stamp me out? Heart by heart? Soul by soul?*

Again came the howl breaking this time into moans so piteous and terrible they seemed the crying of a multitude rather than one.

"Come now, sit with us. Eat and drink," said the young man.

"Let me go to her—your sister."

I staggered ahead, moving beyond his attempts to steady me.

The woman was bound in the litter. Beside the tent, the

litter, roofed and veiled, shook as though the ground beneath moved it.

The shrieks and howls cut the very air.

Younger brothers gathered beside the older who'd given me the water.

"I know you," said one of them. "You're Yeshua bar Joseph, the carpenter. You were at the river."

"And I you," I said. "Ravid bar Oded of Magdala." I moved closer to the litter.

It seemed unthinkable a human could make such sounds. I looked past the tasseled and gathered curtains of the litter.

"Holy Man, if only you can help her—." It was a woman who spoke. She approached with two younger women. Beyond stood the bearers of the litter, muscled slaves with their arms folded, watching, and there too the servants with the horses tethered together.

"My lord," said the woman, "I beg you, she's not clean."

I moved past her. I stood before the giant canopied litter and I opened the curtains.

She lay on a nest of pillows, a woman in her prime, her gaunt body sheathed in linen robes, and her brown hair soaked in sweat and crushed in a great nest beneath her. The stench of urine was overpowering.

Bound from neck to toe in leather thongs, her arms bound out as if to a cross, she strained and seethed in her rage, her teeth cutting deep into her lip. She spit the blood into my face.

I felt it hit my nose and my cheek. Then came her spittle, coughed up from deep within her throat and spewed at me.

"Holy Man," cried the woman beside me. "For seven years, she's been this way. I tell you there was never a more virtuous woman in Magdala."

"I know," I said. "Mary, mother of two, and they were lost with her husband at sea."

The woman gasped and nodded.

"Holy Man," said the brother Ravid. "Can you help our sister!"

The woman on the bed convulsed and her scream ripped through the air, and then the howl, the perfect howl that I'd heard on the mountain. His howl. It cracked again into laughter.

You think you can take her back from me? You think after seven years you can do what no Priest of the Temple has ever been able to do! Fool. They will spit on you for your antics, spit as she spits.

In a sudden spasm of rage, she rose up, breaking the thongs that held her arms. The brothers and the women drew back.

She was bone and sinew and cold fury.

Rising as high as she might, breaking the bond around her neck with a snap, she hissed at me: "Son of David, what have you to do with us? Get away from us. Leave us."

The brothers were aghast. The women crowded together.

"Never, my lord, has she ever spoken in all these years. My lord, the evil one will kill us."

The straps around her breasts broke. The litter, large as it was, rocked on the level ground, and suddenly, with a violent thrust, she broke the remaining thongs that held her legs together. She rose up, crouched, and sprang, knocking back the frame of the canopy, and she rushed out into the open air, falling into the sand and rising to her feet with the swiftness of a dancer.

She gave forth an exultant cry. She spun round terrifying her brothers and the women.

The older brother, the one who'd come to me with the water, rushed to take hold of her. But the younger shouted, "Micha, let him speak to her."

She swayed, laughing, growling like a beast, and then she

almost fell, her legs wobbling, and as she reached for me, her arms revealed themselves, covered in welts and bruises. Her face for one moment was a woman's face and, then again, the visage of an animal.

"Yeshua of Nazareth!" she bellowed. "You seek to destroy us?" She crouched and pitched the sand at me in fistfuls.

"Say nothing to me, unclean spirits," I answered. I bore down on her. "I drive you out, in the name of the Lord on High, I say, Go out of my servant Mary. Go out and away from this place. Leave her."

She arched her back as she rose. But another scream brought her forward as though it were a chain anchored inside her.

Again I declared it, "In the name of Heaven, leave this woman!"

She went down on her knees, her mouth wet and shivering with her panting breaths. She clutched her waist as if holding herself together. Her entire body trembled, and when she shook her fist at me it was as if her hand were being held by another, and she with all her will fought for her own gesture. "Son of God," she bellowed, "I curse you."

"Out of her, I say, all of you. I banish you!"

She twisted this way and that, uttering cry after cry. "Son of God, Son of God," she said over and over. Her body pitched forward and her forehead hit the sand. Her hair fell to reveal the nape of her neck. The sounds coming from her were weakened, anguished, imploring.

"Out of her, all of you, one by one, one through seven!" I declared. I drew in closer, all but standing above her. Her hair covered my feet. She reached out, as if blind, and seeking a hold.

"By the power of the Most High, I say obey me! Leave this child of God as she was before you came into her!"

She looked up. Her hands went out again, but this time so that she might stand, and stand she did, jerked upward suddenly as if pulled by the hair.

"Out I say, one through seven, I drive you out now!"

One more scream rent the air.

And then she stood motionless.

A shudder passed through her, long and natural and filled with pain. And slowly she sank down and lay back on the sand, her head to the side, her eyes half closed.

Silence.

The women began to cry desperately, and then to beg in frantic prayers. If she was dead, it was the will of God. The will of God. The will of God. They approached fearfully.

As Ravid and Micha drew up at my side, I lifted my hand.

In a soft voice, I said:

"Mary."

Only the quiet—the moaning of the wind, the rattling of the palm branches, the gentle ruffling of the silken curtains of the litter.

"Mary," I said. "Turn to me. Look at me."

Slowly, she did as I had asked.

"Oh, merciful Lord," Ravid said in a low voice. "Dear merciful Lord, this is our sister."

She lay as one awakened from a dream, faintly stunned and musing, eyes passing over those who stood around her.

I sank down on my knees and I put out my arms, and she received me. I drew her up close to me. She made no sound, but clung to me as I kissed her forehead.

"Lord," she said. "My Lord."

Ravid's hoarse broken crying was the only thing in the stillness that surrounded us.

. . .

I DOZED.

I saw them, and felt their hands, but I didn't resist them.

The slaves washed me with great luscious streams of water. I felt the old robe taken away. I felt the water worked into my hair. I felt it run down my back and shoulders.

Now and then my eyes rolled up. I saw the golden linen of the tent snapping in the wind. On went the washing.

"Some soup, my lord," said the woman beside me. "Only a little for you have been starving."

I drank.

"No more. You sleep."

And beneath the tent I did.

The desert cooled, but I never lacked for robes or blankets. Soup again, take this, and then sleep. Soup, just a taste. And then their voices far off collected in gentle agitation.

Morning came.

I watched it with one eye from this silken pillow. I saw it rise and push the darkness up and up until the darkness was gone and the whole world was light, and the shade of the tent was cool and sheltering.

Ravid stood before me.

"My lord, my sister has asked to come to you. We ask that you come home with us, that you allow us to care for you until you're well, that you stay with us under our roof in Magdala."

I sat up. I was clothed in linen robes, robes trimmed in embroidered leaf and flower. I wore a soft bleached mantle with a thick border.

I smiled.

"My lord, what can we do for you? You have given back to us our beloved sister."

I put out my arms to Ravid.

He knelt down and held me fast. "My lord," he said. "She remembers now. She knows her sons are dead, that her husband is dead. She has wept for them and she'll weep again, but she's our sister."

He renewed his invitation. Micha had come and he too pressed me.

"You're weak, my lord, you're weak though the demons obey you," said the older brother. "You need meat and drink and rest. You've done this wondrous thing. Let us restore you."

This one, Micha, got down on his knees. He held a pair of new sandals in his hands, sandals studded with brilliant buckles. And he did now what I'm sure he'd never done in all his life as a man. He buckled these sandals to my feet.

The women stood apart. In their midst stood Mary.

She came forward step by step, as if ready at any moment for me to forbid it. She stopped a few feet from me. The rising sun was behind her. She was clean and wrapped in fresh linen robes, her hair bound beneath her veil, her face still for all its scratches and fading bruises.

"And the Lord has blessed me, and forgiven me, and brought me back from the powers of darkness," she said.

"Amen," I said.

"What shall I do to repay you?"

"Go on to the Temple," I said. "That was the direction of your journey. You'll see me again. You'll know when I need your assistance. But for now, I must be on my way. I must return to the river."

She didn't know what this meant, but the two brothers did. They helped me to my feet.

"Mary," I said to her again, and I reached for her hand. "Look. The world is new. You see?"

Faint smile.

"I see it, Rabbi," she said.

"Embrace your brothers," I said. "And when you see the beautiful gardens of Jericho, stand there and look at the gardens around you."

"Amen, Rabbi," she said.

The servants brought me the tightly wrapped bundle of my ruined clothes, my broken sandals. They broke me a walking stick.

"Where do you go?" asked Ravid.

"To see my kinsman John bar Zechariah at the river . . . northward. I have to find him."

"Be quick and be careful, my lord," said Ravid. "He's made the King very angry. They say his days won't be very many."

I nodded. I embraced one after the other of those present, the brothers, the women, the slaves who'd bathed me. I raised my hand in farewell to the wary bearers who stood in the shade of the palms.

There were offers of gold, offers of food, offers of wine for the road. I took nothing, except a final, delicious drink of water.

I looked down at my new tunic and my splendid robe. I looked at the finely crafted sandals. I smiled. "Such soft clothing," I whispered. "I've never seen myself dressed in this manner."

Dry hiss of the desert wind.

"It's nothing, my lord, it's the least, the very least," said Ravid, and the others joined their declarations with his and he repeated them.

"You've been too kind to me," I said. "You've dressed me as I should be dressed, because I'm on my way to a wedding."

"My lord, eat slowly and very little each time," said the woman who'd fed me. "You are gaunt and feverish."

I kissed her fingers and nodded.

I started northward.

24

As before, the air of jubilation gripped those at the river, encompassing the pilgrims who came and went. The crowds were even larger than before, and the number of soldiers had greatly increased, with bands of Romans standing here and there, and many of the King's soldiers watching warily, though no one seemed to take notice of them.

The Jordan was flowing swiftly here and full. We were just south of the sea.

My cousin John sat on a rock beside the stream, and watched his disciples as they baptized the kneeling men and women.

Suddenly John looked up, as if pulled out of his thoughts by some sudden realization.

He looked across the river at me as I came walking along slowly, slipping through the porous crowd, my eyes fixed on him.

He stood and pointed his finger.

"The Lamb of God!" he cried. "The Lamb of God who takes away the sins of the world."

It was a trumpet blast turning every head.

My younger cousin John bar Zebedee gave over the conch from his hands into John's hands.

I held the eyes of John bar Zechariah for a moment. I glanced slowly, deliberately, at the masses of soldiers to my left and then at those to my right. John lifted his chin. He gave a small nod. I returned the nod.

A shiver passed over me. A darkness rose as if the distant mountains had climbed Heavenward and blotted out the sun. The gleaming river was gone. The radiant face of John was gone. My heart was cold and small. But then it grew warmer and I felt it beating. The sun struck the water again and set it afire. John bar Zebedee and another disciple were coming towards me.

The crowd thundered with its usual eager and happy voices.

"Where are you lodging, Rabbi?" asked John bar Zebedee. "I'm your kinsman."

"I know who you are," I said. "Come and see. I go to Capernaum. I go to lodge with the toll collector."

I kept walking. My young cousin deluged me with questions. "My lord, what is it you want us to do? My lord, we are your servants. Tell us, Lord, what do you want of us."

I answered all this with a soft laugh. We had hours before we would reach Capernaum.

Now my sister Little Salome lived in Capernaum. She was a widow with a little son, and lived with her husband's family, who were kin to us and to Zebedee. And I wanted to go to her.

But when we reached Capernaum, Andrew bar Jonah who had come along with John and me from the Jordan now went to tell his brother Simon that they had indeed found the Messiah. He went off to the edge of the sea, and I followed him. I saw his brother Simon bringing in his boat, and with him was Zebedee, John's father, who had John's brother James in the boat with him.

These men were startled by Andrew's excited words.

In the silence, they stared at me.

I waited.

Then I told James and Simon to follow me.

They came at once, and now Simon begged me, please, to come to his house because his mother-in-law was sick with a fever. Word had already reached the sea that I'd driven demons out of the famous demoniac of Magdala. Might I surely cure this woman?

I went into the house and saw her lying there, just sick enough not to care whether or not her children were making noise around her—talking to her of a holy man, and words spoken with great weight at the Jordan River.

I took her hand. She turned and looked at me, annoyed at first that someone would disturb her in this way. Then she sat up.

"Who said that I was sick? Who said that I should be in this bed?" she asked.

And immediately she rose and scurried around the little house, heaping pottage into bowls for us, and clapping her hands for her maidservant to bring us fresh water. "Look at you, how thin you are," she said to me. "Why, I thought I recognized you when you walked in, thought I'd seen you somewhere, but I've never seen anyone like you." She put the bowl of pottage in my hands. "Eat a small bit of that or you'll be ill. It will catch in your throat." She glared at her son-in-law. "Did you tell me I was sick?"

He threw up his hands and shook his head in wonder.

"Simon," I said as we sat down. "I have a new name for you. Peter is your name from this day forward."

He was amazed. He was still speechless. He could only nod.

John immediately sat at my side. "And will you give us new names, Rabbi?" he asked.

I smiled. "You're too eager, and you know it. Have patience. For the moment, let me call you and your brother the Sons of Thunder."

I took the old woman's advice. I ate only a little of the pottage. Hungry as my body was, it did not seem to want more than that.

We all sat on the floor here, cross-legged as usual. I forgot completely from time to time about the fine clothes I wore, which were already dusty, and I looked at Simon who said he must get back now to his fishing.

I shook my head. "No, you're to be a fisher of men now," I said. "You come with me. Why do you think I gave you a new name? Nothing in your life will be the same now. Don't expect it to be."

He looked astonished, but his brother nodded vigorously to him. I lay back and dozed as they discussed all these things amongst themselves. Now and then I watched them as if they couldn't see me. Indeed, they couldn't guess what I was seeing. It was like opening a book, and reading the contents, to know as much as I wanted to know about each and every one of them.

There was a crowd gathering outside the door.

My sister Little Salome had come, the dearest and closest to me of all my kindred. It was a nagging pain to me that she had gone to live in Capernaum.

I was still half asleep when her kiss woke me. Her eyes were deep set and lively and spoke of an intimacy that I shared perhaps with no one in this world, except my mother. Even the shape of her arm in my fingers, the touch of her shoulder against me, these things brought back cascades of memories and unutterable tenderness.

For a long moment I merely held tight to her. She drew back and eyed me in a wholly different way than she ever had

before. She, too, seemed lost for a moment in a string of rec-
ollections. Then I realized she was committing to memory
what she saw of me now, the changes in my expression, in my
demeanor.

Her son came in, bushy headed and curious—the image
of my uncle Cleopas, her father—though he was only a
boy of six.

"Little Tobiah!" I kissed him. I'd seen him on the last
pilgrimage but only briefly in Jerusalem, and that seemed an
age ago.

"Uncle," he said to me. "The whole world is talking
about you!" There was something playful in his eyes so like
his grandfather's.

"Hush now," said my beloved sister. "Yeshua, look at you!
You're thin to the bone. Your face is shining, but you must be
in a fever. You come now home to us, and let me care for you,
until you can go on."

"What, and not be there for Avigail's wedding on the
third day?" I laughed. "Do you think I won't be there for
that? Surely you know all about it—."

"I know that I've never seen you as you are now," she said.
"If it isn't fever, what is it, Brother? Come, stay with me."

"I'm hungry, Salome. But listen. I go on an errand. And I
take these men with me, these men who've come here with
me. . . ." I hesitated, then, "I have one night to spend here
only before we leave for the wedding and I go to find the
toll collector. I'll dine with him tonight under his roof. This
cannot wait."

"The toll collector!" John bar Zebedee was immediately
agitated. "You can't mean Matthew, the toll collector at the
customs post here. Rabbi, he's a thief if there ever was one.
You can't dine with him."

"A thief, even now?" I asked. "Didn't he confess his sins
and go into the river?"

"He's at the customs post, hammering away as he always did," said Simon. "Lord, dine with me under my roof. Dine with your sister. We'll dine with you wherever you like, we'll camp by the sea; we'll dine on my catch. But not with Matthew, the toll collector. Everyone will see and know this thing."

"You don't owe this to him, Yeshua," said Salome. "You do this because our beloved Joseph died in the toll collector's tent. But you don't have to do it. It's not required."

"I require it," I said gently. I kissed her again.

She laid her head against my chest. "Yeshua, there've been so many letters from Nazareth. There's been word from Jerusalem. You're being watched with expectation, and with reason."

"Listen to me," I said. I didn't want to let her go. "You go now and ask your father-in-law if you might come with us to Nazareth to celebrate the wedding of Reuben and Avigail. You and this little one, Tobiah, who hasn't seen his grandfather's house, our house. I tell you, your father-in-law will say yes to this. Bundle up your wedding garments, and we'll call for you both at dawn."

She started to object, to say the inevitable, that her father-in-law needed her, and would never permit it, but the words died on her lips. She was overcome with excitement, and giving me one last kiss, she snatched up Little Tobiah and hurried with him out of the house.

The others followed me.

When I stepped outside the door, there was a young man staring at me anxiously. He was vigorous and covered with dust from his work, but with ink stains on his fingers.

"They're talking of you," he said, "up and down the shore. They're saying John the Baptist pointed to you."

"Yours is a Greek name, Philip," I said. "I like your name. I like all I see in you. Come and follow me."

This gave him a violent start. He reached for my hand but waited for me to give him leave to take it.

"Let me call my friend who's here in the city with me."

I stopped for a moment. I saw his friend in my mind's eye. I knew this was Nathanael of Cana, the student of Hananel I'd seen in Hananel's house when I went to talk to him. In a nearby yard, behind whitewashed walls, the young man was packing his parchments and scrolls and clothing for the journey home to Cana. He'd been all this time working near the sea, and now and then peering at the Baptist from afar. His mind was heavy with worries; he thought this trip home a nuisance, yet he couldn't miss the wedding. He had no expectation that Philip was rushing towards him as he wrestled with his wares and his cares.

I went on down the road, marveling at the numbers who were following us, and the children coming to peer up at us, and the adults who struggled to control them, though they whispered to each other and pointed. I heard my name. Over and over again, they spoke my name.

Nathanael of Cana caught up with us right before we came to the busy road, just opposite the toll post, where the bustle of travelers slowed and gathered in a knot.

There was now a large shuffling idle crowd around us. People moved in to glance at me, and say, yes, that is the man they saw at the river, or yes, that is the man who brought the devils out of Mary of Magdala. Others said, no, it was not. Some declared the Baptist was about to be arrested for the crowds he was drawing, and others insisted it was because the Baptist had angered the King.

I stopped and bowed my head. I could hear every word spoken, I could hear all words spoken, I could hear the words just about to break from parted lips. I let this fall into silence, into the sweet wind rising off the distant sparkling sea.

Only the proximate sounds returned—Simon Peter was declaring that I had cured his mother-in-law by the mere touch of her hand.

I turned my face to the moist breeze. It was lovely and light and filled with the airy scent of the water. My parched body was drinking the water from the very air. I was so hungry.

Far behind us, I knew that Philip and Nathanael were in some sort of argument, and once more I let myself hear what others right beside me could not hear. Nathanael was unwilling, and refused to be moved along against his inclinations. "From Nazareth?" he said. "The Messiah. You expect me to believe this? Philip, I live a stone's throw from Nazareth. You're telling me the Messiah is from Nazareth? What good could come from Nazareth! Man, you are saying impossible things."

My cousin John had turned back to join them.

"No, but truly, he is," declared my young cousin. He was so fervent, so filled with awe, as if he still stood bathed in the miracle of the river, bathed in the Spirit that had visited the waters at the moment the sky had opened. "He is the one, I tell you. I saw it when he was baptized. And the Baptist said, the Baptist himself spoke these words . . ."

I stopped listening. I let the wind swallow their dispute. I looked at the distant gleaming horizon in which the pale hills merged with the blue of the Heavens, and the clouds were borne along as if they themselves were the sails of ships.

Nathanael had come up to me, warily, eyeing me as I nodded to him, and as we fell in stride with one another.

"Ah, nothing good can come from Nazareth?" I asked.

He blushed.

I laughed.

"Here is an Israelite in whom there's no Jacob," I said. I

meant by that he had no guile. He had said what was on his mind without cleverness. He'd spoken from his heart. I laughed again lightly.

We moved into the sluggish crowds on the road.

"How do you know me?" Nathanael asked.

"Ah, well, I could tell you I know you from the house of Hananel where you lately saw me, the carpenter."

This astonished him. He couldn't believe I was that very man. He could scarcely remember that very man, except that because of that man's visit, he'd written a great many letters for Hananel. Slowly these thoughts connected for him, the frail and common carpenter who'd come that day, and now he stared at me, at my eyes, particularly my eyes.

"But let me tell you more truly how I know you," I said. "I saw you just now under the fig tree, alone, and cross, and murmuring to yourself, stacking your unwieldy books and bundles for tomorrow's journey, so perfectly annoyed that you have to be going home for the wedding of Reuben and Avigail when you felt certain that something better, something more important, was likely to happen to you, here, near the sea."

He was shocked. He was for a moment frightened. John, Andrew, James, and Philip made a little circle around him. Peter stood apart. They all watched him uneasily. I could only laugh again under my breath.

"Do I not know you?" I asked.

"Rabbi, you are the Son of God," Nathanael whispered. "You are the King of Israel."

"Because I saw you in my mind's eye, beneath the tree, fretting about so many bundles to take to the wedding?" I thought for a moment, then trusting my mind and my words, I said, "Amen, amen. You too will see the sky opened as John saw it. Only you will not see a dove when you see it opened. You'll see the angels of the Lord on High coming and going on the Son of Man."

I touched my chest with my hand.

He was awestruck. So were the others, but they were caught in a collective fascination, an ever-increasing wonder.

We had reached the toll post.

There sat the rich toll collector whom I'd seen in the river, the man so well described to me as the one who'd taken my beloved Joseph up and away from the bank, the one who'd taken Joseph's body home to Nazareth for burial.

I came up to him. Those waiting to confer with him stood back. Soon the crowd was too large and too pressing, and filled with more than casual rumblings. Horsemen, donkeys laden with goods, carts filled with baskets and baskets of fish—all these waited and people began to fuss that they had to wait.

My new disciples clustered around me.

The toll collector scribbled in his book, his teeth set, lips slightly tensing with the strokes of his pen. Finally, ripping himself unwillingly from his calculations for the shadow at his elbow that would not leave, he looked up and saw me.

"Matthew," I said. I smiled. "Did you write down in your fine hand the things that my father, Joseph, told you?"

"Rabbi!" he whispered. He stood up. He couldn't find any words in his own mind for the transformation in me, for the whole range of small differences he now perceived. The finely woven robes were the smallest part of it. Fine robes to him were a usual thing.

He didn't notice the others who shrank from him. He didn't notice John and James bar Zebedee glowering at him as if they wanted to stone him, or Nathanael eyeing him coldly. He stared only at me.

"Rabbi," he said again. "Had I your leave, I would write

them down, yes, all the stories your father told me and more too, more of what I myself saw when you went into the river."

"Come follow me," I said. "I've been in the desert for many many days. I would dine with you tonight, I and these my friends. Come, make a feast for us. Let us come into your house."

He walked away from the toll post without so much as looking back and took me by the arm and led me into the thick of the little seaside city.

The others wouldn't hurl insults at him, not in his presence. But surely he heard the casual judgments issuing from those behind us, and those who spread out and followed loosely in a small herd.

Without letting go of me, he sent a boy ahead to tell his servants to prepare for us.

"But the wedding, Rabbi," asked Nathanael, plainly distressed. "We must go or we won't be there in time."

"We have the time for this one night," I said. "Don't you worry. Nothing could keep me from the wedding. And I have much to tell you tonight of what happened to me when I was out in the wilderness. You know full well, all of you, or soon will, what happened when I went to be baptized in the Jordan by my cousin John. But the story of my days in the desert is mine to tell you."

25

THE VIOLET EVENING was shining over the hills as we slipped unnoticed into Nazareth.

I had taken us round to where we wouldn't be seen, because the torches were already going up and one could hear the eager voices. The bridegroom was expected within less than an hour. The children were playing in the streets. Women in their finest white robes were waiting already with lamps. Others were still gathering flowers and making garlands. People were coming in from the groves round and about, their arms filled with branches of myrtle and palm.

We found the house in a welter of excited preparation.

My mother cried out when she set eyes on me, and flew into my arms.

"And you thought he wouldn't be here," said my uncle Cleopas, who bound us both in his embrace.

"Look, here, whom I've brought for you," I said, and gestured to Little Salome who at once went into a flood of tears in her father's arms. Little Tobiah. The nephews and cousins came to cluster about us, the little ones to pick at my new garments and all to welcome those whose names I hastily spoke.

My brothers greeted me, each eyeing me a little uneasily—especially James.

All knew Matthew as the man who'd mourned with them for Joseph. No one questioned his presence, least of all Uncle Alphaeus and Cleopas, or my aunts. And his habitual fine clothes created no stares.

But there was no time for talk.

The bridegroom was coming.

Dust had to be fiercely brushed from our clothes, sandals wiped, hands and faces washed, hair combed and anointed, wedding garments taken out of their wrappings, Little Tobiah to be scrubbed like a vegetable and garbed immediately, and so we lost ourselves in the preparations.

Little Shabi ran in to announce that he had never seen so many torches in Nazareth. Everyone in the entire village had turned out. The clapping had begun. The singing.

And through the walls we could hear the thump of the timbrels, and the high-pitched melodies of the horns.

Not a glimpse of my beloved Avigail.

At last we went out into the courtyard, all we men to be ranged around it. Out of the baskets, the little ones took the exquisitely made garlands of ivy and white-petaled flowers, and placed a garland on every bowed head. Yaqim was with us. Silent Hannah in shining white, her maiden hair gracefully combed beneath her veil, held up the garland for my head, her eyes brimming as she smiled.

I looked at her face as she turned away. I heard the music as she heard it, the insistent beat. I saw the torches as she saw, flaring without a sound.

The twilight was gone.

The light of lamps and candles and torches was dazzling as it flashed and flickered in the lattices and on the rooftops across the way.

I could hear the singing rising with the strum of the harp

strings, and the deeper throbbing of the strings of the lutes. The very crackling of the torches mingled with the singing.

Suddenly the horns sounded.

The bridegroom had reached Nazareth. He and the men with him were coming up the hill to joyful salutes and great volleys of clapping.

More torches flared suddenly in the yard around us.

Out of the central doors of the house came the women in their bleached woolen robes, beautifully banded in bright colors, their hair wrapped up in their finest white veils.

Suddenly the great white linen canopy festooned with ribbons was unfolded and hoisted. My brothers Joses, Judas, and Simon and my cousin Silas held the poles.

The street before the courtyard exploded with joyful greetings.

Into the torchlight stepped Reuben, garlanded, and beautifully robed, beaming, his face so filled with gladness that my eyes swam with tears. And beside him, the eager friend of the bridegroom, Jason, who sought now to present him in a ringing voice:

"Reuben bar Daniel bar Hananel of Cana is here!" Jason proclaimed. "For his bride."

James stepped forward, and for the first time, I saw beside him the hulking, grim-faced Shemayah, the garland slightly askew on his head, his wedding garments not quite reaching their proper length due to the great width of his shoulders and the thickness of his immense arms.

But he was there! He was there—and he pushed James forward now towards the excited and explosively happy Reuben who came into the courtyard with open arms.

Silent Hannah rushed to the doorway of the house.

James took the embrace of Reuben.

"Joyous greetings, my brother!" James said loudly so that all the crowd beyond could hear it, and the clapping answered him fiercely. "Joyous greetings as you come into this the house of your brothers and to take your kinswoman as a bride."

James stepped to the side. The torches moved in towards the door of the house as Silent Hannah stepped out and gestured for Avigail to come forward.

And come forward she did.

Swathed in veil upon veil of Egyptian gauze, she stepped into the flaring illumination, her veils encrusted with gold, her arms ornamented with gold, her fingers with glistening and multicolored rings. And through the thick and shimmering mist of white cloth, I could see the distinct glimmer of her dark eyes. The mass of her dark hair fell down over her breasts beneath these veils, and even on her sandaled feet were great rounded and glittering jewels.

James raised his voice:

"This is Avigail, daughter of Shemayah," he said, "your kinswoman and your sister, and you take her now with the blessing of her father and her brothers and her sisters, to be your wife, in the house of your father, and let her from now on be a sister to you, and may the children you have be as brothers and sisters to you, according to the Law of Moses, and as it is written, let this be done."

The horns sounded, the harps throbbed, and the timbrels beat faster and faster. The women lifted their timbrels now to join the resounding rhythm of those from the street.

Reuben stepped forward as did Avigail, until they stood before each other beneath the canopy, the tears coming silently from Reuben as he reached for the veils of his bride.

James put his hand between the two figures.

Reuben went on speaking to the face he could see distinctly now just in front of him, beneath its sheer drapery.

"Ah, my beloved," he said. "You were set apart for me from the beginning of the world!"

Shemayah was pushed forward by James until he stood at the shoulder of the young groom. Shemayah looked at James as if he were a trapped man and would flee if he could, but then James whispered to him to urge him and Shemayah spoke:

"My daughter is given to you from this day forward and forever," he said, glancing uneasily at James who nodded. Then Shemayah continued: "May the Lord on High guide you both and prosper you both on this night and grant you forever mercy and peace."

Before the shouts of jubilation could silence him, James pitched his voice loud and clear:

"Take Avigail to be your wife in accordance with the law and decree written in the Book of Moses. Take her now and bring her safely to your house and your father. And may the Lord and all the Court of Heaven bless you on your journey home and through this life."

Now came the new and uncontrollable inundation of clapping and cheering.

The women closed ranks around Avigail. Jason drew Reuben back and out of the courtyard with all the men following, except for my uncles and brothers. The canopy was folded only to make it narrow enough to pass through the gateway, and the bride, flanked by all the women of the house, including Little Mary and Little Salome and Silent Hannah, proceeded, with Avigail beneath the canopy. Once in the street the canopy was opened again.

The drone of the horns rose above the faster, more furious thumping of the harp strings. The wooden flutes and pipes rose in sweet, rousing melody.

The whole party moved down past the lighted doorways and the radiant faces, and the clapping hands. Children ran ahead, some carrying lamps dangling from poles. Others carried candles, hugging the flames against the breeze with their tiny hands.

The women lifted their timbrels. Out of yards and doorways came others with their harps and their horns and their timbrels. Here and there came the rattle of the sistrum, the jingling of bells.

Voices rose in singing.

As the crowd reached the open road to Cana, we all beheld the unbelievable spectacle of the torches on either side of us, lining the way, for as far as we could see. Torches moved towards us from the distant slopes and through the dark fields.

The canopy was now spread to its full width. Flower petals were hurled in the air. The music grew stronger and quicker, and as the bride continued, in her phalanx of women, the men on either side, up ahead and behind, began to lock arms and dance.

Reuben and Jason danced to the left and the right, arms locked, one foot stepping to the side over the other, then back again, swaying, gesturing, singing to the rhythm of the music, their outside arms raised above their heads.

Long lines formed to flank the procession, and I fell in, dancing with my uncles and my brothers. Little Shabi and Yaqim and Isaac and the other young ones pivoted and leapt in the air, and clapped their hands heartily.

And with every step, with every turn, we saw the road ahead still ablaze with a wealth of welcoming light. More and more torches approached. More and more villagers joined our ranks.

And so it was until we poured into the enormous rooms of Hananel's house.

He rose from his couch in the great dining room to greet his grandson's bride with open arms. He clasped the hands of James and Shemayah.

"Come in, my daughter!" Hananel declared. "Come in

this, my house and your husband's house. Blessed be the Lord who has brought you to us, my daughter, blessed be the memory of your mother, blessed be your father, blessed be my grandson Reuben. Come in now to your home! Welcome, with blessing and joy!"

He turned now and led the way past the blazing candelabra, for the bride and all her women to enter the dining room and other chambers set apart for them, where they would feast and dance, to their heart's content. Linen veils, trimmed in purple and gold and bound with purple and gold tassels, came down to separate the women from the men in the many archways of the banquet room, veils through which laughter and song and music and gaiety could penetrate, while giving the women the freedom to be pale shapes beyond the eyes of boisterous and roaring men.

Under the high ceilings of the house, the music exploded. The horns vied with the pipes in melodies, and the timbrels sounded as before.

Huge tables had been set throughout all the main rooms, round which couches were prepared for Shemayah and all the men of his daughter's family who had come with him, and for Reuben, and for Jason, and for the Rabbis of Cana and of Nazareth, and for a great flock of men of distinction, all beloved of Hananel, all of whom we knew and did not know.

Through the open doorways, we saw great tents spanning the soft grass, and carpets spread everywhere, and tables at which everyone might gather, either on couches or right on the rugs, whichever they desired. Amid all, the candelabra burned with hundreds upon hundreds of tiny flames.

Great platters of food appeared, steam rising from the roasted lamb, the glistening fruit, the hot spiced cakes and honey cakes, the piles of raisins and dates and nuts.

Everywhere, men and women turned to the water jars, and to the servants beside them, to rinse their hands.

A great row of six jars stood in each banquet room. A row of six stood out beneath each tent.

The servants poured the water over the outstretched hands of the guests and offered the clean white linen cloth for drying, catching the old water in silver and gold basins.

The music and the aromas of the rich platters melded and it seemed for a moment to me that—as I stood in the courtyard, in the very middle of it, staring from one feasting group to another, gazing even at the chaste veils that divided us from the dancing figures of the women—I was in a great unbroken universe of pure happiness which no evil could ever approach. We were as a vast field of spring flowers united in one gentle current of tender breeze.

I forgot myself. I was nothing and no one except part of it.

I moved outside, through the ranks of the dancers, past the busy and beautifully laden tables, and I looked—as I always do, as I've always done—for the lamps of Heaven on high.

It seemed to me then that the lamps of Heaven were even here the deep and private treasure of every single soul.

Could I not die now? Could I not dissolve this skin and rise as I'd so often thought of it, weightless and brimming, into the company of the stars?

Oh, if only I could indeed stop time, stop it here, stop it forever with this great banquet, and let all the world come here to this, now, streaming, out of Time and beyond Time, and into this—to join with the dancing, to feast at these abundant tables, to laugh and sing and cry amid these smoking lamps and twinkling candles. If only I could rescue all these, in the midst of this lovely and embracing music, rescue all these—from the blooming youth to the ancient with their patience and their sweetness, and their flush of unexpected and ravishing hope? If only I could hold them in one great embrace?

But it was not to be. Time beat on as the heels of the hands beat the membrane of the timbrels, as the feet stamped the marble, or the soft yielding grass.

Time beat on, and in time, as I'd told the Tempter, yes, as he'd tempted me to stop Time forever—in time, there were things yet unborn. It struck a deep dark shiver in me, a great cold. But it was only the shiver and fear known to any man born.

I did not come to stop it, I did not come to leave it at such a moment of mysterious joy. I came to live it, to surrender to it, to endure it, to discover in it what it was I must do, and whatever it was, well, it had only begun.

I looked around me at the many moist and ruddy faces. I saw Young John and Matthew, and Peter and Andrew, and Nathanael—all of them dancing. I saw Hananel weeping as he clasped his grandson, Reuben, who offered the cup to him to drink, and Jason embracing both of them, Jason so happy, so proud.

My eyes drifted over the whole assembly. Unnoticed I walked through room after room. I walked under the tents. I walked through the courtyard with its huge standing candles, and its high anchored torches. I peered over my shoulder at the soundless masses of gathered women beyond the veils.

I let my mind go before me. It went where the man could not go.

Avigail, veil lifted now that she lay among the children of the bridal chamber only, with Silent Hannah seated on the couch at her feet. Avigail, her eyes closed, as she slept.

I saw in my mind's eye just as clearly and simultaneously that instant in the courtyard at home when Reuben had said to her, "My beloved, you were set apart for me from the beginning of the world."

My heart filled with pain; it was washed in pain.

Farewell, my blessed darling.

I let the grief come. I let it run through my veins. It was not grief for her, but for the absence of her forever, the absence of that intimacy, the absence of that one beating heart that could have been so very close. I let myself know it in the absence, and then I kissed her with all my heart on her tender forehead in the image I held of her, and I let this go. Leave me, I said to this. I can't take you where I am going. I always knew that I couldn't do it. And I let you go now, yes again and for always—I let go of the wanting, I let go of the losing, but not the knowing . . . no, I will never let the knowing of it go.

An hour before dawn Reuben was led to the bridal chamber.

The women had already taken Avigail to the bridal bed. It had been strewn with flowers. Veils of gold surrounded the bed.

Jason embraced Reuben with one last hearty clap of his hands on his shoulders.

And as the door closed behind Reuben, the music found a new delirium, and men danced ever more quickly and with greater spirit, even the old men rising, and some who could barely do it without the hands of sons and grandsons; and it seemed the whole house was once again filled with the earliest and loudest cries of joy.

People were still streaming in from the countryside. They gave away their rustic amazement with wide wondering eyes.

Tables had been set out on the grass for the poor of the villages, and platters of hot bread and bowls of meat pottage were being put out for them. Beggars had been brought in—

some of the very lame, who generally gathered at the outside gates of such a banquet hoping for the scraps.

Beyond the veils the long chain of dancing women swayed to the left, step after step after step, then stopped, whirled, and rocked on their feet. Chains of male dancers passed me winding in and out of the arched doorways, round about the central table, behind the proud grandfather who leaned now on Jason's arm. Nathanael sat beside Hananel, and Hananel for all the wine he'd drunk was hammering Nathanael with questions while Jason smiled and dreamed as if it did not matter at all.

Here and there, men glanced at me, especially some of the newcomers, and I heard their confidential questions. *Is he the one?*

All night I'd been hearing this, if I wanted to hear it. All night I'd caught the turning heads, the quick furtive stares.

Suddenly I sensed that something was wrong.

It was like hearing the first rumble of a storm when no one else hears it. It was that moment when one is tempted to reach out and say, "Be quiet. Let me listen."

But I didn't have to say those words.

I saw now at the far end of the dining room the servants in frantic argument with one another. Two more of the household servants joined with the others. More frantic whispers.

Hananel heard it. He gestured for one of them to come, and whisper the cause of this in his ear.

Shocked, he turned, and struggled to climb to his feet, dismissing Jason who tried halfheartedly and drowsily to assist him. The old man went to the servants. One of them disappeared into the room of the women, and came back again.

Now other servants were gathering. Yes, something was very wrong.

From out of the curtained privacy of the women's banquet room, my mother appeared. She moved along the margins of the room, unnoticed, her eyes lowered, ignoring the drunken men as they danced and laughed in their habitual fashion. She was heading towards Cleopas, her brother, who sat at the large table opposite Hananel's couch. Hananel himself was still in heated argument with his servants, and his pale withered face was turning red.

My mother touched her brother's shoulder. He rose at once. I saw them searching for me.

I stood in the courtyard in the very center of the house. I stood against the candles as I had for a long time.

My mother came to me, and put her hand on my arm. I saw panic in her eyes. She glanced at all the company round, the hundreds gathered under the roof and outdoors in the tents, at those who nudged each other and laughed and talked at the tables quite oblivious to the distant knot of servants, or the expression on my mother's face.

"Son," she said. "The wine is running out."

I looked at her. I saw the cause of it. She didn't have to tell me. The caravan carrying the wine south had been struck on the road by brigands. Cartloads of wine had been stolen, carried off into the hills. Word had only just reached the house, even as dozens of men and women still arrived for the banquet which would go on throughout all of the new day.

It was a disaster of unlikely and dreadful proportions.

I looked into her eyes. How urgently she implored me.

I bent down and laid my hand on the back of her neck. "Woman?" I asked gently. "What has this to do with you and me?" I shrugged. I whispered, "My hour hasn't come."

She drew back very slowly. She looked up at me for a long moment with the most curious expression on her face, a combination of mock scolding and then placid trust. She turned and lifted her finger. She waited. Far across the court-yard and the main dining room, one of the servants saw her, caught her gaze and her gesture. She nodded, as he nodded to her. She beckoned. She opened her fingers. She beckoned for all of them to come.

Hananel was suddenly standing alone without his servants, watching them slip through the crowds and come towards us.

"Mother!" I whispered.

"Son!" she answered, gently mimicking my very tone.

She turned to Uncle Cleopas and put her hand gently on his shoulder, and gazing up at me out of the corner of her eye, she said to Cleopas, "Brother, tell my son the commandment. He has lately received the blessing of his father. Remind him. 'Honor your father *and* your mother.' Are those not the words?"

I smiled. I bent to kiss her forehead. She lifted her chin slightly, eyes soft, but withholding her smile.

The servants surrounded us. They waited. My new followers were gathering—John, James and Peter, Andrew and Philip. They'd never been very far from me the whole evening and now they drew in close.

"What is it, Rabbi?" John asked.

Far away, the small figure of Hananel stood with folded arms in the candlelight, staring at me, fascinated and perplexed.

My mother pointed to me, as she addressed the servants: "Do whatever he tells you to do."

Now her face was gentle and natural and she looked up at me and she smiled as a child might smile.

The disciples were confused and concerned.

Cleopas laughed silently to himself. He covered his mouth with his left hand, and peered up at me mischievously. My mother walked away. She gave one sharp backward glance at me, her face sweet and trusting, and then she retreated to the door of the women's banquet room and there she waited, half hidden by the gathered curtains in the arch.

I looked at the six huge limestone jars in the courtyard, the jars for the water of the purification, the washing of hands.

I spoke to the servants. "Fill them to the brim."

"My lord, they hold gallons. It will take all of us to take these to the well."

"Then best to hurry," I said. "And call the others to assist."

At once they hoisted the first of the jars and carried it out, through the rear dining room into the night. Another flock of servants appeared for the second, and another group for the third, and so on it went rapidly, so that within minutes the six stood as before, completely filled.

Hananel watched all this carefully, but no one was watching him. People passed him, greeted him, thanked him, blessed him. But they didn't really notice him as he stood there. Slowly he moved back to his place at the table. He sat down, coming between the merry conversation of Nathanael and Jason. His eyes were still fixed on me.

"My lord, it's done," said the first of the servants as he stood beside the row of jars. I gestured to a nearby tray of goblets, only one of many throughout the room.

I heard in my mind the voice of the Tempter in the desert. *A delusion! . . . Why, even Elijah could have managed that!*

I looked at the head servant. I saw the tension and near desperation in his eyes. I saw the fear in the faces of the others.

"Draw now from the jar and fill that cup," I said. "Take it to Jason, the friend of the bridegroom who sits beside the master. Is he not the master of the feast?"

"Yes, my lord," the servant answered wearily. He put the dipper into the jar. He let out a long low gasp.

The red wine shone in the light of the candles. The disciples stared as the wine flowed down from the dipper into the goblet in the servant's hand.

I felt the coolness come over my skin that I'd felt at the Jordan River. I felt a faint near-delicious sizzling sensation. Then it was gone as quickly and silently as it had come.

"Take it to him," I said to the servant. I pointed to Jason.

My uncle was unable to laugh, or speak. The disciples seemed to collectively hold their breath.

The servant hurried into the banquet room and around the table. He thrust the goblet into Jason's hand.

I let the words reach me through the noise of the throng.

"The wine that's just come," said the servant, trembling, almost unable to form the words.

Jason took a deep drink of it without hesitating.

"My lord!" he said to Hananel. "You've done the most splendid trick." He stood up. Drank more from the cup. "Most men wait until the first wine's done its work, only to bring out the lesser vintage. You've saved the best wine for last."

Hananel stared up at him.

In a small cold voice, he said,

"Give me that cup."

Jason didn't notice the coldness. He was already arguing with Nathanael again, but Nathanael was staring across the table and beyond, at those of us gathered in the courtyard by the jars.

Hananel drank. He sat back. We looked at one another over the distance.

The servants were hurrying to the jars and ladling the wine into the empty cups and goblets. Tray after tray was being taken to the banquet tables and rugs.

No one saw Hananel looking at me, except for Nathanael. Nathanael rose slowly and came towards us.

Out of the corner of my eye, I saw my mother leave her post at the door of the banquet room and disappear behind the thin veils of gauze.

Young John kissed my hand. Peter knelt and kissed my hand. The others gathered to kiss my hand.

"No, stop this," I said. "You must not do this."

I turned and I went out of the courtyard, through the foyer, and into the open garden away from the revelers. I walked until I was in the farthest corner of the walled orchard from which I could see the rooms of the women flanking this side of the house. The arches were filled with pulsing light.

All the disciples were now clustered around me. James headed towards me and so did my younger brothers.

Cleopas came and stood before me.

Jason and Nathanael and Matthew came out, Matthew arguing forcefully with Young John and with one of the servants, a very young boy, who fell back now, shyly, bowing his head and backing away.

"I tell you, I don't believe it!" said Matthew.

"What do you mean, you don't believe it!" declared Young John. "I saw it. I saw them take the jars to the well. I saw them bring the jars back. I talked to them. I saw their faces. I saw it. How can you stand there and say you don't believe it?"

"That explains how you believe it," said Jason, "but not how we are to believe it." He rushed up to me, forcing the others out of the way. "Yeshua, do you claim to have done this, to have changed those six jars of water into wine?"

"How dare you put that question to him!" said Peter. "How many witnesses does this require for you to believe? We stood there. His uncle stood there."

"Now, that I do not believe," declared my brother James. "Cleopas, did you witness this yourself, what they're saying, that all the wine being served now was water before he changed it? I tell you, this is mad!"

Suddenly all but Cleopas were speaking at once. Only Cleopas stood there studying me.

The night was evaporating and up came the deepest blue of the dawn. The stars, my precious stars, were still visible. And beyond, the house sang still and throbbed with dancing.

"What will you do now?" Cleopas asked.

I thought for a long moment. Then I answered.

"I will go on, from surprise to surprise."

"What are you saying?" James demanded.

They fell to quarreling again. Jason gestured furiously for silence. "Yeshua, I demand that you tell these gullible fools that you did not turn water into wine."

My uncle began to laugh. As was always the way with him the laughter started low, creeping, and then gathered strength and depth. It remained muted yet became darker and fuller.

"Tell them," said James. "Our young cousin here will make himself a laughingstock with this story. He'll make you a laughingstock with it. Tell them this did not take place."

"It did take place, we saw it," said Peter. Andrew and James bar Zebedee joined furiously in the affirmation. Then my brother James threw up his hands.

"I believe you could drive the devil out of a woman," said Jason. "I believe that you can pray for the rain to stop and it might stop. Those things, yes, I believe those things. But not this, this I don't accept."

Cleopas spoke up again.

"What will you do?" He drew very close to me, so that I couldn't escape him, but the others could still hear him.

"When you were a little boy, you asked me many a time for answers. Remember this?"

"Yes."

"I told you one day you would give us the answers. And I also told you that I would explain everything that I knew."

"Yes."

"Well, I am telling you now: you are the Anointed One. You are Christ the Lord. And you must lead us."

Peter, the sons of Zebedee, and Philip all nodded and said they too believed this.

Cleopas said, "You must lead us now, you have no choice. You must go forth and answer every challenge put to Israel. You must take up arms as the prophets have foretold."

"No."

"Yeshua, you can't escape it," Cleopas said. "I saw and heard at the Jordan. I saw the water changed into wine."

"Yes, these things you saw," I said, "but I will not lead our people into battle."

"But look around you," said Jason hotly. "The times demand it. Pontius Pilate—why, he's the reason John came out of the wilderness. It was Pilate with his cursed ensigns. And the House of Caiaphas, what did they do to avert the disaster! Yeshua, you must call all Israel now to take up arms."

"My brother," said James. "Surely that is so."

"No."

"Yeshua, the words of Isaiah call on you to do this," said Cleopas.

"Don't quote them to me, Uncle. I know them."

"Yeshua, if you did this thing," said James, "then how can we fail? We must take up arms. It's the moment we've waited for, prayed for. If you tell me you did this—."

"Oh, I know how bitterly you are all disappointed," I said. "And I have seen in my mind's eye the armies I might lead and the victories that might come to pass. How could you think I don't know such things?"

"Then why won't you accept your destiny?" asked James bitterly. "Why must you always step back?"

"James, don't you understand what I want? Look into the faces of those around you who saw the wine come from the jar. I want an innovation that will ignite the world. That wine is no less than the blood inside my veins. I come to bring the Face of the Lord—to the whole wide world!"

They fell silent.

"The Face of the Lord," I repeated it. I looked intently at James, and at Cleopas. I looked one by one at each of them. "The Face of the Lord I mean to bring to all."

Silence. They stood still loosely gathered and staring at me, rapt yet not daring to speak.

"Don't you know all battles fought with swords are ultimately lost battles?" I asked. "Don't you see yourselves that Scripture and history are filled with battles? What comes of battles? Don't speak to me of Alexander or Pompey or Augustus, of Germanicus or any Caesar. Don't speak to me of ensigns whether they are raised on high in Jerusalem or lost in the Teutoburg Forest of the far north. Don't speak to me of King David or of his son Solomon. Look at me as I stand here! I want a victory that far surpasses anything that's been written, either in ink or in blood."

I went on speaking against their silence.

"And you must trust in me how I will do it," I said. "Whether in signs and wonders, whether in moments of personal calling, whether in pointed and trivial or enormous demands! I call on you to follow me. To discover it with me."

No answer.

"It begins now at this wedding," I said. "And the wine you've drunk is for the whole world. Israel is the vessel, yes.

But the wine flows from now on for all. Oh, I wish I could fix this as the final triumph, this lovely morning with its gentle paling sky. I wish I could open the gates for all to come and drink of this wine here and now, and that all pain and suffering and suspense would come to an end.

"But I wasn't born for that. I was born to find the way to do this through Time. Yes, it is the Time of Pontius Pilate. Yes, it is the Time of Joseph Caiaphas. Yes, it is the Time of Tiberius Caesar. But those men are nothing to me. I've entered history for the whole of it. And I won't be stopped. And I go now, disappointing you, yes, and to what village and town I head next, I don't know, only that I go proclaiming that the Kingdom of God is on us, that the Kingdom of God is with us, that all must turn and take heed, and I will declare it where the Father tells me I must, and I will find before me the listeners—and the surprises—He has in store."

"We are with you, Master," whispered Peter.

"With you, Rabbi," said John.

"Yeshua, I beg you," James said softly. "The Lord gave us the Law on Sinai. What do you mean—do you mean you will go now to roam through villages and towns? To cure the sick by the side of the road? To work wonders such as this in a tiny hamlet like Cana?"

"James, I love you," I said. "Believe in me. Heaven and earth were made for you, James. You'll come to understand."

"I fear for you, Brother," he said.

"I fear for myself," I said. I smiled.

"We are with you, Rabbi," said Nathanael. Andrew and James bar Zebedee said the same. My uncle nodded, and let the others come between us with their clamoring, their outstretched arms.

My mother had appeared sometime during all of this and she stood far off, listening perhaps, or simply watching. I did not know. Little Salome, my sister, was there, with sleepy Little Tobiah by the hand.

Beyond them and far to the left, on the farthest margin of the garden away from us, amid a small grove of shining trees, there stood a tiny robed figure with her back to us, rocking from side to side, her veiled head bowed.

Tiny and alone, this dancer, seemingly watching the rising sun.

Little Salome came forward. "Yeshua, we must go home now to Capernaum," she said. "Come with us there."

"Yes, Rabbi, come back to Capernaum," said Peter.

"We'll go with you wherever you go," said John.

I thought for a moment and then I nodded. "Get ready to leave," I said. "And those of you who will not, we must say, for now, our farewells as best we can."

James was brokenhearted. He shook his head. He turned his back. My brothers clustered around him in perplexity and misery.

"Yeshua," said Jason, "do you want me to come with you?" His face was filled with innocent urgency.

"Can you give up all you have, and follow me, Jason?" I asked.

He stared at me, blankly. And then slowly he frowned and looked down. He was hurt and torn.

I looked away again at the small distant figure.

I motioned for them to stay behind me here and I went across the garden towards her, the little dancer who appeared to face the light rising above the wall.

I walked the full length of the house, past the curtained rooms of the women. I walked over the scattered petals where earlier many had danced.

I came up behind the little figure who was swaying with the thump of the distant drums.

"Hannah!" I said.

She started. She turned around. She looked at me, and then her eyes moved in all directions, up to the birds in the tree branches above her, to the doves chortling on the tiled roof. She stared at the house, still so full of light and movement and noise, lovely insistent rhythmic noise.

"Hannah," I said again and I smiled at her. I put my hand to my chest. "Yeshua," I said. I opened my hand and pressed it to my heart. "Yeshua."

I placed my hand gently on her throat.

She struggled, eyes wide, and then she whispered it:

"Yeshua!" She was pale with shock. "Yeshua!" she said hoarsely. Then loudly. "Yeshua." *Yeshua, Yeshua, Yeshua.*

"Listen to me," I said as I put my hand on her ear and then on my heart—the old gestures. " 'Hear O Israel,' " I said, " 'the Lord Our God is One.' "

She started to say it. I repeated it, this time with the gestures she'd seen us make for her as we prayed it every day. I repeated it once more and then the third time she spoke the words with me.

Hear O Israel. The Lord Our God is One.

I held her in my arms.

And then I turned to join the others.

And we started for the road.

A NOTE ON THE TYPE

THIS BOOK was set in Adobe Garamond. Designed for the
Adobe Corporation by Robert Slimbach, the fonts are based on
types first cut by Claude Garamond (c. 1480–1561). Garamond
was a pupil of Geoffroy Tory and is believed to have followed
the Venetian models, although he introduced a number of
important differences, and it is to him that we owe the letter we
now know as "old style." He gave to his letters a certain elegance
and feeling of movement that won their creator an immediate
reputation and the patronage of Francis I of France.